GEOFF NICHOLSON

Geoff Nicholson has been hailed as a witty and acute writer for his novels STREET SLEEPER, THE KNOT GARDEN, WHAT WE DID ON OUR HOLIDAYS, HUNTERS AND GATHERERS, THE FOOD CHAIN and THE ERROL FLYNN NOVEL. The sequel to STREET SLEEPER, STILL LIFE WITH VOLKS-WAGENS, will be published in paperback by Sceptre in 1995. Geoff Nicholson is also the author of two works of non-fiction, BIG NOISES and DAY TRIPS TO THE DESERT. He lives in London.

Geoff Nicholson

STREET SLEEPER

British Library C.I.P.

A CIP catalogue record for this title is available from the British Library

ISBN 0 340 613254

Printed and bound in Great Britain for Hodder and Stoughton Ltd, a division of Hodder Headline PLC, 338 Euston Road London NW1 3BH by Cox & Wyman Ltd.

For Tessa.
For Les, who is not fat.
For Helena, who made me go part-time.
For Steve, who makes the roads safer.
For Andy, who gets run down.

One

There is a garage in a railway arch. It is in darkness. In that darkness coils of hose hang like rubber intestines; stacks of tyres slouch like rolls of matt, black fat. The floor is stained a hundred shades of black and brown, each shade the colour of oil. Workbenches, floor and walls are jagged with body-panels, metal innards, girlie calendars and fast-food wrappers.

It's not much but it's home to Fat Les. A sign above the arch announces 'Fat Les – the Vee-Dub King'. He works here. He lives here. He sleeps in a partitioned area that he calls his office. He is in his forties; fat (of course), unshaven, sweaty. His bed is a tartan sleeping-bag. He does cheap servicing, tuning and repairs of Volkswagen Beetles. He knows most of what there is to know about flat-four, air-cooled engines. He makes a living, more or less, and pumps any profits into his hobby which is playing around with flat-four, air-cooled, Volkswagen engines.

In the centre of the garage sits his own unimposing car. It is a light blue Beetle, an early seventies model. It is starting to rust badly, apparently well past its best, and its best apparently never anything special. One thing's for certain – it's not much to look at.

In her parents' end of terrace house in Gleadless, Barry Osgathorpe's fiancée, Debby, said to him, 'What are those, pet?'

'Nerf bars,' he replied.

1

There were two nerf bars sticking out of the shopping-bag he was carrying.

'Pardon?' said Debby.

'They're cast-iron, T-shaped pieces of metal used to replace the front and rear bumpers on a Volkswagen Beetle. They look really flash.'

'I'm sorry, pet, I don't think I'm quite with you.'

'Look, Debby, I've got a confession to make. I've been taking driving lessons in secret, and I've passed my test.'

'Well that's very nice, but why in secret?'

'I don't really know.'

But he did really know.

'And I've bought a car as well.'

'Aren't you the sly one? That's smashing. It'll come in ever so handy after we're married. When can I see it? I'm sure I'll like it.'

She was wrong.

'It's no good,' Barry Osgathorpe said, 'we shan't ever be married because I've decided that I must go out "on the road" and find myself.'

Later he said, 'Call me Ishmael. That's not my real name, of course. Barry Osgathorpe is a good enough name for a librarian, which until now I have been content to be. But now I style myself a Zen Road Warrior and I feel in need of a change.

'So call me Ishmael.'

Sometimes Fat Les dreams of building a car that runs on water, on air, on grass, earth, carbon monoxide, on urine – only for his own benefit, you understand. He doesn't want to make a million, not even a profit, more important he doesn't want to hear the knock on the garage door, the visit of the assassin from the oil-producing country.

He has been sitting behind the wheel of his car for some

2

time now, sitting in silence, in readiness, preparing himself. Now he starts the engine. Headlights tunnel through the darkness. The car slides gently, steadily out of the garage and on to the street. He drives cautiously and correctly to the main roads. There is no hurry. There is nothing to prove. Not yet.

It was three days since Ishmael had abandoned Debby and left home. It was getting dark. He was driving out of the services at Newport Pagnell in a customized Volkswagen Beetle – not very well customized at that – frenched headlights, a whale tail, smoked glass, nerf bars.

He sat back on the faded leopardskin seat covers and pressed down the accelerator.

And then he saw her. She was blonde. She was standing at the side of the exit ramp. She was wearing high heels, a short fur coat, a leather skirt and a tee-shirt with diamanté. Her thumb was out. All his life he'd been waiting for a moment like this. He stopped the car. He opened the door.

'Well met, fellow-traveller,' he said.

'How far are you going?'

'Further.'

'Will you see me all right for Leicester Forest East?'

He could see she was not yet in the mood for any cosmic truths. He nodded. She got in. She slammed the door. They drove off.

She was younger than she had looked. The mascara was thick and cracked, the high heels scuffed, her stockings had a ladder. The blonde hair could have been a wig.

Still, she was beautiful in her own way.

Everybody is.

'Some motor,' she said.

'I call it Enlightenment,' Ishmael replied, 'because that's the only vehicle worth owning. I'm looking for a Way, a Clearway, no stopping, no U-turns, no reversing. I want the headlights to pick out the Truth. That's the only road you should think of hitching a lift on.

'And that's why I drive up and down the motorways, the arterial routes, the B-roads, roads where a man might lose himself, where a man might find himself. Perhaps I'm something of an outlaw, perhaps a pariah. I like to think of myself as a pilgrim. I'm trying to make a little progress.'

'That's nice,' she said.

'Of course, I wasn't always like this. I used to be a librarian. Then one day I was doing a local author display when the scales fell from my eyes. It was what you might call a satori.'

'Yeah.'

'Yes. I was all set to be married and settled but something told me I was on the wrong road. Debby, my betrothed, was a bit cheesed off naturally, but you know how it is, I had to be free to journey to the centre of myself.

'But here I am talking about myself all the time. How about you? What wisdom do you have to share with me?'

'Eh?'

'Well, what do you do?'

'Me? I get into cars with strange men, then I tear my clothes . . .'

She made a savage rip in the diamanté tee-shirt. One small, freckled breast popped out through the rip.

'Then I threaten the driver that unless he gives me money I'll go to the police and swear that I've been raped.'

What is a Street Sleeper?

You pull up at a red traffic light. You are driving a black Ford Capri. The stereo pumps out eighties' funk. You burned-off an ailing Jag at the last set of lights. You are at home behind the wheel of your car. You are safe. You are accommodated.

4

The lights stay red for a long, long time, and as you tap your fingers on your leather steering-wheel, as you blip your engine, you become aware of another car pulling alongside. Maybe it's competition.

You look. It isn't. It isn't even worth your derision. It is a Volkswagen Beetle, an early seventies model in pale blue except where it is pitted with rust, and where the wings are bubbling with virulent corrosion.

You are well aware that there are some hot Volkswagens on the streets, cars with hot-rodded engines, fancy extractor-type exhausts, low profiles on Wolfrace slots, but this . . .

It is not worth a first glance. It is beneath your contempt. What kind of clown drives a car like that?

You look. You see what kind of clown. The driver is a fat, unshaven, sweaty man in his forties. His hair, an overgrown short-back-and-sides, has settled round his head like a tight, greasy cap, framing a face made ragged years ago by acne; a series of chins like deflated tyres, a loose mouth that will not stay shut.

He wears a snug, filthy shirt that clings to his fat shoulders and belly. The sleeves are pushed up above squat forearms that end in broad, spatulate hands, bitten nails, thick fingers stained with oil.

And perhaps that is the first clue, the first indication that all may not be quite what it seems. Could those be mechanic's hands? Could they have been assembling and fitting performance accessories, adjusting clearances, greasing nipples?

The second clue, the last you will need or be allowed, as the lights turn at last to amber, is the quiet sure sound of a mighty engine, a silencer that shouts its intentions loud and clear, a rising yet calm note of awesome torque and acceleration. And even though you release the Capri's clutch and your car starts to leap forward before the appearance of the green light, you are instantly trailing in the wake of the Beetle, in the wake of the Street Sleeper.

You are angry, not only that you are beaten at your own game, though God knows that's bad enough, but more because you have been beaten by a player you didn't even know was in the game, who, in that poxy little blue Beetle, certainly didn't have any *right* to be in the game.

The evening is in tatters. The girl beside you refuses to sympathize, even suggests that you see the funny side. The night will end in a furious row, dredged up grievances, thrown drinks and broken lager glasses.

All of which is much as Fat Les had intended. He drives his car through dark streets that hold no threat, not even that much of a challenge these days, a heftily rebored engine, racing cam, forged pistons, and twin Webbers have seen to that. He doesn't feel smug exactly, but content that, this time at least, the underdog, the wimp in the white hat, the loser, has won.

He drives back to his railway arch, to his kingdom. A remote-controlled solenoid operates the doors. He drives in, switches off engine and lights. He drinks a lot of cheap whisky and watches snooker on television before sliding into his sleeping-bag and into chivalric dreams.

He dreams of conquest, of winning. Burning-off Ford Capris is part of it (actually, quite a large part), but is not the whole story. It is a symptom. Of social unrest? Of class hatred? Fat Les couldn't put a name to it. But it is indicative of his desire to defeat the flash bugger, the boy-racer, the wine drinker, the one with the tasty motor that can move a bit, the one in Daddy's BMW, the one in the car that Daddy bought him for his eighteenth birthday. It is the parading of a chip on the shoulder. It is also a way of saying do not take me for a sheep, not even for a wolf dressing down, do not take me for anything at all. Do not judge me. Fat men in old bangers need love too.

*

When Ishmael first decided to drive off and find out who he truly was, he'd envisaged buying a VW camper with cooker, washbasin and portable toilet. It seemed simple and good. It also turned out to be expensive.

He answered a classfied ad in the *Morning Telegraph*. The camper had been sold before he got there, but the seller was a small-time dealer and he said he had another car which might suit Ishmael down to the ground.

It was, of course, the car that he came to call Enlightenment.

Ishmael was shown the car. It was the ugliest thing he'd ever seen. The front spoiler and rear whale tail were in grey primer. Most of the rest of the car was painted in candy red and that would have been nice enough but it had started to crack, and rust was showing in a few places. However, not all the car was painted that colour. One rear wing was black and dented, the other was bright orange, and the driver's door was lilac with a peeling transfer of a Viking on it.

It had a sunroof without a hatch – and that was when Ishmael first started to feel an affinity with the car. How nice to sit in the driver's seat, open to the wind and sky, open to new thoughts and experiences. Just open.

And he realized how there is beauty in ugliness, and he saw how the many colours of paintwork symbolized the rich, chequered patchwork of life.

Slowly but clearly the car spoke to him. And he spoke back.

He started the engine. It needed a few attempts but at last it sprang into life. There was a dense cloud of blue smoke from the exhaust. The dealer told him this was a good sign. Ishmael settled himself in the car. Man and machine started to communicate. A connection was made. A deal was done.

He had his mission. He had his vehicle. He had the few thousand pounds he'd drawn out of the joint account he'd opened with Debby. He paid the dealer in cash. The man kept chuckling to himself. Ishmael smiled back.

He drove away from the life he knew.

It was the first step on the road to coming home.

'Oh,' said Ishmael. 'Tearing your clothes and screaming rape seems like a strange calling, but who am I?'

The blonde with the freckled breast said, 'You don't seem to understand. That's what I do. That's what I'm doing now.'

Ishmael was silent.

'You want me to give you money?' he said at last.

'You've got it.'

He was silent for a while longer.

'Have you ever heard of the concept of karma?'

'What?'

'Doing bad things is going to give you terrible bother in your future lives.'

She suddenly lost her patience.

'All right, stop the car or I'll leap out and tell the police you threw me.'

Even though it meant disobeying the Highway Code Ishmael brought the car to a sudden halt on the hard shoulder.

'Money isn't the answer,' he said.

'For *you* at this moment money *is* the answer. Unless you give me some money you're going to be in a lot of trouble – and soon.'

She stuck her head out of the car window and screamed. It was a piercing enough scream but Ishmael had heard louder ones from Debby, and in any case there was nobody to hear. The sound of one vocal cord screaming.

'Let's talk this thing through,' Ishmael said.

She screamed again. Cars roared past. Ishmael pressed a button on the dashboard. It controlled the windows.

8

They slid shut with an electronic rasp. He pressed another button and both doors were now locked. There was still the gaping hole where the sunroof ought to have been but he couldn't see her escaping through there.

Ishmael abhorred violence in all its many ugly forms, so it was with great reluctance that he now reached down under his seat and picked up a claw hammer. He held it about an inch and a half from the blonde's nose.

'What's your name?' he asked.

'What are you going to do with that hammer?'

'I'm going to use it in the service of virtue.'

'Oh yeah?'

'So tell me what your name is.'

'Marilyn.'

'OK then, Marilyn, it seems to me you're not a very good person. Oh, I don't imagine you're actually evil, not wicked exactly, but perhaps you haven't had all the advantages that someone like me has enjoyed. But fortunately I'm now in a position to help you.

'This claw hammer will serve a moral purpose. Either you behave yourself and stop demanding money with menaces from me, or you continue to do wrong in which case I hit you across the mouth with the hammer.

'It's sort of like the wrath of God, only more immediate.'

'I'm an idiot,' she said quietly to herself. 'The moment I saw the car, obviously a nutcase.' Then aloud. 'All right, you win. Let me out and I won't give you any more trouble.'

'No, Marilyn. You and I are going to take a ride. This will be a learning experience for you.'

Munich, 1922. Two children press their faces against the glass of a Benz motor showroom. Inside, vast and luxurious motorcars stand ready to be bought by the rich and ostentatious. Jacob Werlin is demonstrating the features of a sixteen-horsepower model to a Herr Weiss and his wife. Weiss is a solid, square, bespectacled citizen. He calls himself an industrialist, which is sufficiently vague to be impressive, though there is nothing vague about his very real wealth. His wife is noticeable for her accessories – a veil, a stole and a dachshund.

The children, a boy and a girl, Nina and Peter, aged six and eight, continue to stare. Werlin sees them but is not immediately concerned. Children love motorcars. Why shouldn't they? He himself retains a boyish fascination. He owes his success as a representative for Benz to an astute combination of business skills and a youthful enthusiasm for speed, power and elegance. But what is the little girl doing? She is pulling faces, tongue out, nose squashed flat against the glass, eyes rolling in a crazed, hostile mime. And the little boy, my God, has his penis out and is peeing against the window.

Herr Werlin tries to interpose his body, to become a screen between his customers and the children. The loss of dignity he would suffer in chasing off a pair of ragged children might result in the loss of a sale.

'Put your breast away,' Ishmael said.

'Are you some kind of pervert?'

'Do I look like one?'

'You can't always tell by looking.'

'Actually, sex is something I haven't got sorted out yet.'

'You don't say.'

'Debby and I had a perfectly good sex life. It was very pleasant but not really spiritual. Or maybe it *was* spiritual, just not all that much fun.'

'Why are you telling me this?'

'Yes, why indeed? We're here to sort out your problems not mine. Tell me your troubles.'

*

In the same building as the Benz showroom is the editorial office of the *Völkischer Beobachter*, the newspaper of the National Socialists. Herr Hitler is often seen entering and leaving the building. Jacob Werlin finds him a nice enough chap, perhaps faintly extreme in his opinions about Jews and communists, but with his heart more or less in the right place. He drives a Benz, or rather his chaffeur does. Herr Hitler too is a motoring enthusiast, although inevitably he sees it from a rather uncompromising political perspective.

Herr Hitler now emerges from the newspaper office, sees the children at the window and delivers sharp, accurate slaps to their ears. The children run, the little boy dribbling as he goes. Herr Hitler enters the showroom.

'Well,' said Marilyn, 'I had a pretty bad childhood if you really want to know.'

'Yes, I really want to know.'

'My mother drank. She wasn't up to the job of motherhood. She was a barmaid when she worked at all. She had sailors in a back room of the pub, on the bare lino. It wasn't a pretty sight.'

'You watched?'

'I had to. We six children all slept in that back room.'

'That's awful.'

'Then there was my father, when he was around, which wasn't often. He was a jazz musician, a drummer. He did some drugs – joybanging he called it. He always said he wasn't hooked. We knew better. He interfered with me, quite often.'

'This is heart-rending,' Ishmael said.

'Of course, I married to get away from my background but it was no good. He was called Carlos. He used to beat me. I discovered on my wedding night that he was a pimp. I had to take on a couple of clients so we could afford to pay for the hotel on our honeymoon.'

11

'I don't think I can stand to hear any more.'

'So are you surprised that I hitch lifts on motorways, tear my clothes and demand money?'

'Good afternoon, Jacob,' Adolf Hitler says.

Jacob Werlin introduces him to the two potential customers.

'The Benz is a fine car,' Hitler says. 'My friend Jacob here sold one to me, not so grand as the one you were looking at, but a fine car even so. It is efficient. It is comfortable, and it is German.'

'It is also expensive,' Herr Weiss says.

Hitler smiles knowingly.

'It is luxurious,' Jacob offers.

'Yes,' Hitler says, 'it is luxurious. At this moment in German history the motorcar is a luxury item, and I suppose that will always be one of the roles of the car, but it need not be only a rich man's status symbol. It isn't that in America. There Henry Ford has made motor transport easily and cheaply available to the ordinary man.'

'You would not have me driving around in a Model T,' Herr Weiss laughs.

'No, I would not. But I wish there was a German car that was as cheap, as reliable and as available as a Model T. It is my opinion there will be such a car. I have one or two ideas myself.'

'You are ambitious, Herr Hitler,' says Weiss. 'A politician, a newspaper man, now an automobile engineer.'

He looks straight into Hitler's laundry-blue eyes, notices the flat, wide, mongrel face, the hair and moustache that signal some form of misplaced bohemianism. And he listens to the harsh but uninflected voice that betrays its owner's unimpressive Austrian origins. And Herr Weiss is deeply unimpressed.

'I have read widely,' Hitler replies. 'I have read recently

some copies of an American newspaper called the *Dearborn Independent*. It is run by Mr Ford. He seems to have one or two sound ideas. I have a copy I could lend you if you are prepared to take an interest, and I suggest you should be. The leading article is entitled "The International Jew – the World's Problem".'

Ishmael was moved.

'I knew there had to be a reason,' he said.

Marilyn was crying quietly.

'I'm sorry to burden you with my problems,' she said.

'No, no, a problem shared. I'm sorry I threatened you with the hammer. It was because you obviously thought I was an easy touch. For ten years in that bloody library everyone thought I was just a wimp, just a nothing. Nobody's ever going to think I'm an easy touch again.'

'I don't think you're an easy touch. I think you're really sweet.'

'Oh,' he said. Nobody had ever said anything like that to him before.

'I don't suppose,' she continued, 'you could see your way clear to lending me twenty quid or so, could you? Just to tide me over.'

'For a fellow-traveller it would be a pleasure. It would be a duty.'

'Thank you. I'm really grateful. They broke the mould when they made you.'

In the end he gave her twenty-five pounds and let her out at the next services. It was dark now. He watched as she walked away from the car towards the brightly lit buildings, the clatter of her high heels audible even after she had disappeared into the blur of lights.

Ishmael sat at the wheel in silence, drinking in the evening, savouring this moment of shared humanity. Then somebody in a Ford Capri sounded his air horns behind him. He was blocking the entrance to the petrol pumps.

The still moment was over. He drove on.
Do not expect to fare well. Only hope to fare forward.

Herr Weiss says, 'I am interested in buying a car, Herr Hitler. I am not interested in hearing the views of an arrogant and ill-informed young man who happens to lead an insignificant workers' party. Jacob, I shall return another time. Perhaps.'

Jacob Werlin shuffles uneasily, attempts a bow of farewell. There is a general movement towards the door but Adolf Hitler moves fastest and blocks the exit. He begins to harangue the departing couple.

'I am well-informed and I am well-educated. A good deal more than yourself. I have studied as an artist and I am a self-taught expert in architecture, military science and engineering. I have served the Bavarian Infantry with honour, and I tell you this: there will be a new Germany. You will see the moral, industrial and military rearmament of our country. You will see new wealth. You will see new buildings, new factories, autobahnen to link place to place and man to man, and you will see a German people's car – an emblem of freedom, mobility and egalitarianism for the German working man. And perhaps then, Herr Weiss, you will remember this conversation, and you will know that I was right. And I shall remember you, with your foolish dog, and your more foolish wife, and you will be sorry.'

At the end of 1923 Herr Weiss reads in his morning paper, and reads with great pleasure, that Adolf Hitler has been gaoled following an attempted putsch against the Weimar government.

'The best place for him,' he says to his wife.

Hitler is imprisoned in Schloss Landberg, but is allowed considerable freedom, receives many visitors and has access to any reading and writing materials he needs.

He particularly enjoys reading *My Life and Work* by
Henry Ford, and he begins work on a book of his own,
called *My Struggle*.

Two

Ishmael's Ten Prerequisites for a traveller.

1. A good heart – yes, it's that simple.

2. A few clean pairs of underpants. (What if he had an accident?)

3. One of those polystyrene cooler things in which you put a little plastic container that's been in a freezer overnight, that keeps things cool for up to twelve hours. (Actually, he soon realized this was not one of his better ideas since you're seldom in a position to put the little plastic container in a freezer when you spend most of your nights sleeping in lay-bys.)

4. Canned goods. Fruit cocktail, corned beef, smoked mussels, steak and kidney pudding, guavas, baked beans with miniature pork sausages, artichoke hearts, Royal Game soup, cling peaches, mandarin segments, Irish stew, and many others.

5. A tin-opener. (He thought of everything.)

6. A blue leather motorcycle suit. (This wasn't strictly a prerequisite, but he felt it added to his image and it was in a sale at Lewis Leathers. So far he hadn't had the nerve to wear it.)

7. A copy of *How to Keep Your Volkswagen Alive – A Manual of Step-by-step Procedures for the Compleat Idiot*. This is the most thoroughly 'right-on' car manual the world has ever seen, its good advice includes tying back your long hair before tampering with the fan-belt. (Ishmael couldn't understand it.)

8. A vibrator with four interchangeable heads – three

of which he couldn't envisage any possible use for, but perhaps he would encounter some warm and wonderful soulmate with whom to explore the possibilities.

9. A copy of Ian Fleming's *The Man with the Golden Gun*. (He knew that it would have been more appropriate to have had some Herman Hesse but it was the only book on the rack at the Watford Gap Services that he liked the look of.)

10. A mind that listens. And a mind that hears. (OK, eleven prerequisites.)

Renata Caswell is writing the editorial for next month's *Cult Car* magazine.

'Why me?' she has already protested. 'Isn't the editor supposed to be in charge of writing the editorial? Or am I being too pedantic?'

'You're being too pedantic,' says Terry, the editor.

She slides a new sheet of paper into her manual typewriter and tries again.

> We here at *Cult Car* believe we cater for the true motoring enthusiast, the true car lover, and we set no hard and fast rules about what kind of car you're allowed to love. Oh, sure, it's easy to love your Jensen, your Austin-Healey, your E-Type, and we've run articles on all those models; but we know that our readers are just as likely to be enthusiastic about Austin A40s, Morris Travellers, even 2CVs. We aim to satisfy those readers too. What we care about is cars with style, cars with soul. Why, take this issue . . .

And then she stops. It isn't easy to take this issue. The freelancers haven't come up with the goods yet. They've been promised one article about a man in Cumbria who has spent several years' wages restoring a Vauxhall Velox to showroom condition and beyond. They're hoping for three thousand words on a Coventry man who claims to have put a Rover V8 into a Datsun Cherry. Those who work on *Cult Car* and who are of a technical frame of mind have variously claimed that this is madness, suicide and impossible. So maybe the three thousand words will never appear. There is a whisper that a Lamborghini Countach is to be delivered so that *Cult Car* can take it for a test-drive, but this is the kind of magazine where nobody ever believes whispers. Then they've been promised a definitive piece on the Ford Edsel, but Terry swears the Edsel is old hat. Renata is not so particular. She is only the 'staff writer' after all. She is paid an hourly rate. She seems to spend most of her working life turning press releases into copy, sometimes improving the grammar, but most often her creative effort comes to no more than retyping.

Nineteen thirty-three, Berlin, Dr Ferdinand Porsche arrives for his four o'clock appointment with Adolf Hitler. He knows that they will be discussing 'motoring topics' and that Herr Hitler has a special interest in small car engineering, a thing that Porsche has worked at desultorily throughout his career. What surprises Dr Porsche is just how specific Herr Hitler's ideas are.

Hitler is not interested in theory. He wants a car designed, or rather he has designed it himself, in his head, and now he just needs someone to concern themselves with the dreary practicalities of production.

The car is to appeal to the German working-class family man, must therefore be able to carry two adults and three children, must be capable of forty miles to the gallon, must be able to sustain high speeds for long periods on the autobahnen, and since the working man will have no garage facilities it must be easy to maintain and must be air-cooled to withstand the rigours of the German winter.

All this Dr Porsche can do, but at a price. Adolf Hitler

names his price: one thousand Marks – about fifty pounds.

Ishmael woke up in a lay-by. He had slept on the back seat of the Beetle. The windows were steamed up. He had twinges in various remote parts of his body. His feet were hot and sticky in his shoes. He had four days' growth of beard and a mouth like a holy man's loincloth.

Still, he thought, it was good to be alive.

What he needed to set himself up was a good English breakfast – bacon, sausages, eggs, mushrooms, fried bread, all moving around in a sea of grease.

He drove back to the motorway. The next services were twelve miles away.

Enlightenment ate up the miles with all the eagerness he would soon be applying to his breakfast. He arrived at the services and parked. He went in through the swing doors. It was early, yet already there were kids playing on the electronic games in the foyer.

Ishmael was saddened.

Dr Porsche, and for that matter the rest of the German motor industry, know that Hitler's plan is more or less impossible. In England William Morris has managed to produce a highly austere and denuded Morris Minor, but even that costs £100.

Porsche must have been aware that even in 1933 one did not tell Adolf Hitler that he was crazy, but he may also have enjoyed the challenge of the impossible, perhaps it may even have been that Porsche and Hitler genuinely shared a benevolent dream of mass mobility and freedom.

'You know another reason why the Edsel was such a failure?' asks Terry.

'Surprise me,' Renata replies.

'Because the automatic didn't have a gear-lever. It had

bloody push buttons. Men and women, they all like to get something thick and meaty in their hand.'

Renata knows *she* does. She is thirty-five, still willing in flesh and spirit, still single, still an enthusiast for fast cars and fast men; and still, though who knows for how much longer, the owner of a driving licence. It has been endorsed a couple of times, which hasn't stopped her driving very fast and occasionally very dangerously, and she does have a clever mouth that runs away from her when talking to fuzz. Her brain is telling her to use her charm while her mouth is calling the nice policeman a stunted fascist.

At the same time she realizes that a motoring journalist who has been banned from driving is a luxury that *Cult Car* would probably force itself to do without.

'I need a drink,' she says.

'And I need that editorial,' says Terry.

A stop on the motorway, Ishmael reasoned, ought to be a chance to stop and reflect on the finer things, a chance to sniff the air, to look at the grass. Yet here in the foyer of the services were kids whose only break from the road was a chance to dice with electronic imitations of death.

Ishmael started to get angry.

What base form of philistinism offers games of death as entertainment? Why couldn't service stations have foyers full of Blake's paintings? There need be no musak – there could be Bach and Bartok playing. Travellers could stand in informal groups and discuss art and philosophy.

He went to a tall youth playing one of the games and tried to explain all this to him. He was about seventeen, skinny, failing to grow a moustache. He had on a studded leather jacket, his breath smelled of juicy fruit gum and he had a ghetto-blaster at his feet.

At first he didn't seem to catch Ishmael's drift so Ishmael held him firmly by the shoulder and tried to take him into the clear morning air where the point could be made with fewer distractions.

They didn't get as far as the clear morning air. The moment Ishmael placed a hand on the boy's shoulder he sprang from the machine and confronted Ishmael in a martial-arts pose.

'Don't ever lay a finger on me,' he said very loudly. 'Don't you ever touch me, you wanker. Nobody ever touches me.'

Ishmael was unsure of his next move. A crowd of youthful low-life was gathering round them. Someone shouted, 'Go on son, hit him. Don't let him get away with it.'

'You see,' Ishmael said after some consideration, 'violence begets violence. You play on that infernal machine and then you transfer that mindless set of violent reactions to real life. You wouldn't have reacted like this if you'd just spent the last ten minutes contemplating Picasso's "Weeping Woman".'

'Go on, stick one on him. He's yellow and he talks funny.'

The youth relaxed slightly but the general body language still spoke of alert aggression.

'What's your name?' Ishmael asked him.

'Davey.'

'Mine's Ishmael.'

There was a whoop of derision from the crowd. It came from the person who had been egging Davey on. He looked old enough to know better. He was wearing a yellow cardigan.

'I think you must be tired of living,' he said to Ishmael. 'I reckon this boy's got deadly weapons for hands.'

'That doesn't surprise me,' Ishmael snapped. 'He seems to have dead matter for brains.'

'You shouldn't talk to a martial-arts expert like that,' said yellow cardigan.

21

'Be reasonable,' Ishmael said. 'I put my hand on somebody's shoulder to show him that there's a world of truth and beauty waiting for him out there and he reacts like a brute beast. What happened to reason? What happened to human fellowship?'

Davey shifted uneasily from foot to foot.

'A lot of people forget there's a large spiritual dimension to the martial arts,' he said.

He slipped his hands into the side pockets of his jacket. Ishmael wondered briefly if he was going to pull a knife. The crowd looked at him expectantly.

'You know,' he said, 'you might have a point. Come on.'

He jerked his head to indicate that Ishmael should follow him outside. They went together.

Terry is probably ten years Renata's junior. He has been performing major surgery on cars since he was ten or eleven, been driving them since long before then, and he has one A-level, though admittedly it is in English.

Renata, by contrast, has an English degree and aborted careers in advertising, radio journalism and arts administration behind her. She wrote her first motoring article after a holiday in Mexico, three years ago.

As your flight touches down in Mexico, as you put aside your copy of *The Boys from Brazil*, and as you gaze out of your aircraft window, your first thought is that you have landed in the centre of a Mexican Volkswagen enthusiasts' meeting.

Teams of cleaners, mechanics, security men and customs officials are ferried to and fro in Beetles that would be thrown out of the average English scrapyard for making the place look untidy.

All the taxis in Mexico City are Beetles, or at least *nearly* Beetles. Most of them lack what you would take to be some vital part – like wings, or a driver's door, or

22

lights, indicators and windscreen. They are held together, not so much with string and chewing gum, more with frayed bootlaces and spit, but under those battered, mutilated, sometimes barely recognizable, exteriors there beats the unmistakable throb of Doc Porsche's favourite flat-four engine . . .

And so on. She met an American with a good suntan and a good camera who took slides of the more spectacularly ruined cars, and on her return to England she sold the article to *Classic Motoring* magazine.

Ishmael and Davey stood in the car-park. There were hills and trees in the distance. There was a grass verge.

'England,' said Davey. 'God's own country.'

Ishmael agreed. He asked where Davey was travelling to and discovered he was going to his married sister in Stoke. A friend of his mother was giving him a lift. The friend was still in the Gents. Davey didn't like his married sister much but it was better than being at home with his mother.

'I think I begin to understand,' Ishmael said. 'This violence you express towards the world, be it vented on an electronic game or on an innocent stranger who tries talking to you about higher realities, this is surely a displaced feeling of anger and resentment that you have for your mother.'

Davey thought long and hard.

'No,' he said, 'I think it's just a phase I'm going through.'

Herr von Opel, head of the largest motor manufacturer in Germany, is present at the signing of the contract whereby Ferdinand Porsche agrees to produce three prototypes, one of which will be developed into the people's car. Von Opel turns to Porsche and sneers, 'What a wonderful contract. Ten months of highly paid futile labour, at the end of which you write a simple memorandum stating that the project is impossible, a fact that those of us with the least intelligence are aware of *now*. How I wish we all had such wonderful contracts.'

Porsche is furious, and that insult to his integrity concentrates the mind wonderfully. Or does he know that he is to be the director of a dream sequence in which everything is possible, except the bargain price? Perhaps the war, with its reshuffling of moral and financial values, will come as a welcome relief. What is unaffordable in times of peace becomes priceless in war, the restaurant menu without prices.

Just to demonstrate good-will Ishmael let Davey show him how to play one of the electronic games, and Ishmael did seem to have a talent for it. First you're driving a futuristic racing car round an intergalactic grand prix circuit, but at intervals the way is blocked by alien monsters and you have to shoot them out of the way, but at other intervals the monsters mutate, you find your weapons are useless and you have to plunge the car into hyperspace. Ishmael got a higher score than Davey. Then Davey's mother's friend came out of the Gents and Davey prepared to leave.

The fellow in the yellow cardigan had watched all this with disapproval.

'I still think you should have stuck one on him, kid,' he said to Davey.

'Hey, do me a favour will you?' Davey replied. 'Piss off.'

Yellow cardigan took out his frustration on a pinball machine. Ishmael went into the dining-room for breakfast. He was feeling damn good at having beaten Davey on the machine. Then as he ate it slowly dawned on him that the little bastard might just possibly have let him win. He felt suddenly hollow.

*

The American with the good camera was called Dick and he insisted on taking Renata to a Mexican live sex show, not that he had to insist very hard. They envisaged a dimly lit stage spread with straw, a big-thighed Senorita fellating a burro. The reality was somewhat different. They sat in a nightclub with expensive drinks in their hands, and watched topless girls dancing behind a smeared glass screen. This went on for longer than anyone could possibly have wanted until Dick asked the waiter when the sex show was going to start. He was told that he had been watching it for the last thirty-five minutes. There were brief, loud protests and a scuffle before Dick and Renata found themselves on the street again, waiters yelling incomprehensible threats after them into the night. A small boy had been watching the episode and asked them if they wanted to watch his mother in a lesbian show. They turned him down. He looked hurt.

'There might have been another article in it,' Renata said later. 'An exposé, something radical, compassionate.'

Or it might have been another rip-off.

She began freelancing on motoring topics with an off-beat or feminine angle. 'Beauties Who Aren't Afraid of Beasts; Renata Caswell talks to four women who drive hard to handle macho machines.' You know the sort of thing.

Then came the offer of a job as staff writer on *Cult Car*. The magazine had been running for just six months, trying to capture the market sector that likes cars but isn't made up of boy-racers or Porsche-fanciers. It was even hoped that some women might buy it. Renata couldn't see it lasting more than another six months, and even if it did she certainly hoped she wouldn't still be with it.

It was a sadder but wiser man who ate his English breakfast that morning. Yes, thought Ishmael, in many ways life is like a computer game, but he didn't go into details.

He thought again of body language. You see a youth standing in front of you in a martial-arts pose, teeth set, nostrils flared, right away it says *aggression*. You see a girl in a magazine – legs splayed, eyes rolled in mock ecstasy, immediately the body language says, 'I'm only doing this for the money.'

Ishmael was lingering over his pot of tea. The place was crowded yet nobody would come and sit next to him. Their body language was telling him something.

He smelled. It was time to do some laundry.

He had always hated laundrettes, not that it mattered much since Debby's mother washed most of his clothes. He suddenly missed Debby, but there was nothing for it. He drove along the motorway until he saw a huddle of new houses just off the road. He took the next exit and drove back. He found a clean, smart laundrette and parked outside.

He would put on his blue leathers and wash all his other clothes. There weren't many. He scrabbled about on the back seat and changed. This was not easy, not in a Volkswagen Beetle, not parked outside a laundrette in the middle of a new housing estate. He was grateful for the smoked glass.

The desire to belong to something more important and greater than ourselves is a very natural, very understandable and very dangerous one.

Within the Nazi Party there were so many groups and sub-groups to which one might belong. The fifteen- to eighteen-year-olds had the Hitler Youth, the younger still had the Deutsches Jungvolk. Girls could join the Bund Deutscher Maedel, women the NS Frauenschaft. There were Nazi organizations for doctors and teachers and civil servants. There was even a place for artists in the Nazi Kulturbund. There was room for everyone. Everyone could be included, more or less. And if you wanted to take part in almost any leisure activity, be it soccer, or chess, or skiing, it was necessary to be a member of a club which was itself a member of, and was directed by, an organization called Kraft-durch-Freude – Strength Through Joy.

Ishmael stuffed his dirty clothes into a pillow-case and entered the laundrette.

A fellow in the corner approached him. Ishmael could tell right away he was not ordinary. He was smoking a wet cigar, which Ishmael found anti-social in the confines of the laundrette, but he didn't complain. He wanted to avoid conflict, at least for the next half hour or so.

The man looked sixty, had grey hair cut into a young style with a Nero-type fringe. He was overweight but tall enough and big-boned enough to avoid being gross. He wore a blazer and a couple of big gold rings. Ishmael's mother would have called him a fine figure of a man.

He said to Ishmael, 'Do you want to share my washer?'

'Pardon?'

'I see you don't have much laundry, and neither do I. Would you care to put your things in with mine? Save money.'

It seemed like a good idea at the time. Hell, thought Ishmael, you hear so much about 'English reserve' yet here he was, a complete stranger, being treated with almost Mediterranean good humour by one of the locals.

'When you're a single man you don't ever seem to create enough laundry for these big machines.'

Ishmael agreed with him. It was only small talk. They weren't having a real sharing of ideas as yet but he had to start somewhere.

There were those, too, who might become members of the SA – Sturm-Abteilung, a storm-trooper, brown shirt. They were close to Hitler, they had their own martyr,

27

Horst Wessel, gone to live in a slum with a prostitute in order to dedicate himself to the Nazi cause, and murdered by communists. But their image was bad – drinkers, street brawlers, homosexuals.

William L. Shirer writes, in *The Rise and Fall of the Third Reich*:

> Many of its top leaders, beginning with its chief, Roehm, were notorious homosexual perverts. Lieutenant Edmund Heines, who led the Munich SA, was not only a homosexual but a convicted murderer. These two and dozens of others quarrelled and feuded as only men of unnatural sexual inclinations, with their peculiar jealousies, can.

Oh really? But it is not surprising that Peter Baldung, a young man of Aryan appearance and with the desire to belong to a winning side, is delighted when instead of becoming a mere SA he can become a Schutzstaffel, SS, a member of Hitler's personal army, with their smart distinctive uniform and their oath of personal loyalty to the Führer. Peter feels he has come a long way since he was that small boy who pressed his face against the glass of the Benz showroom in Munich all those years ago.

'Love the leather suit,' the man said.

'It's the first time I've worn it, actually. It's a bit warm.'

'My name's Howard by the way.'

'Call me Ishmael.'

The man looked puzzled at first.

'Oh, as in Moby *Dick*.'

And then he laughed in a way that Ishmael found incomprehensible and a bit coarse.

They sat for a while and watched the laundry go round.

'It's very outlaw.'

Ishmael assumed he was still talking about the leather suit.

'It was in a sale.'

They continued in this disconnected way for some time until, out of the blue, Howard said, 'Look, do you give or take?'

At last, Ishmael thought, they were getting down to some spiritual basics.

'I do both,' he said. 'Naturally. It seems to me that if there's one basic thing that would make the world a happier place it's a genuine bit of give and take.'

Ishmael got the impression that Howard had stopped listening, an impression confirmed when he jumped to his feet and started to pace the laundrette.

'Look,' he said in a loud whisper, 'my place is just round the corner. Let's go and have a stiff gin and tonic.'

Gin and tonic at ten in the morning! This was real Bohemianism. Poor old Debby. She thought two Baby-chams and a bag of pork scratchings were the first steps on the road to becoming an absinthe drinker. His mother too. If he'd suggested anything more extreme than a glass of sherry on Christmas morning she'd have thought he was the Antichrist. How far he had come.

By 1944 Peter Baldung will be a trusted high-flyer at Buchenwald, an intimate friend of Frau Ilse Koch, wife of the commandant there, also known as the Bitch of Buchenwald. Peter will learn to put up with her tantrums, her hysterical whims, and will aid her in her new hobby of making lampshades from human skin. He will seek out for her skin that is young, healthy, unblemished by age or disease. But the first time he offers her a skin that is smooth, clear but also embellished with a tattoo of a matador, she is beside herself with delight. She is thrilled beyond all reason.

But in 1935 Peter is merely part of the retinue that accompanies Adolf Hitler to a race meeting at Avus, along with Jacob Werlin who is now Hitler's official adviser on motoring matters. Werlin and Hitler have had no chance to talk, indeed Hitler has not been able to speak to anyone, having lost his voice after some intensive oratory. But Hitler is keen to know the latest details of Dr Porsche's developing Type 30. They slip into the garden of a local Reichskanzlei and Hitler summons Peter. He commands him to turn around and he uses Peter's broad black, uniformed back as a writing desk. On a piece of paper Hitler jots down urgent questions about the project. How many horsepower has the engine? Air-cooled? Weight of car? Is the test model ready?

Before Ishmael could say, 'What about my laundry?', Howard was out of the door. Politely, Ishmael follow-ed. He offered Howard a lift in Enlightenment. He declined.

'I'm afraid I have to be discreet,' he said.

Ishmael shrugged. He had no idea what Howard was talking about.

Howard's flat was, Ishmael supposed, actually quite nice. To be honest, it wasn't really to his taste. It seemed a bit middle class. It smacked too much of materialism. He knew that was a terrible thing to think about anyone but he would have had to say what he thought.

There was a rattan three-piece suite and a nest of rattan tables with glass tops. There were lots of art deco bits and pieces – lamps in the shape of boy shepherds, a clock with an enamel sunset, and a cocktail cabinet with carved fauns for legs. There were more mirrors on the walls than anyone could possibly find any use for, art books were spread around conspicuously, and there was a massive collection of videotapes.

Howard mixed a potent gin and tonic.

Werlin answers Hitler as best as he can. Peter listens intently to it all even though he cannot know what questions are being asked, but above all he feels proud to be of such a direct use to the Führer.

Ishmael was sitting in a rattan chair looking out of the window on to a patch of communal lawn when Howard drew the curtains.

'Too, too bright,' he said.

Ishmael was about to encourage him to let the sun shine in, but Howard said, 'Do you like this table?'

He pointed at the largest of the glass-topped tables. Ishmael didn't like it especially, but he saw no reason to be hurtful.

'It's fine,' he said.

'It's my very favourite,' Howard said, chuckling. 'If this table could talk . . .'

By now Ishmael was convinced that Howard was raving. He just wanted to get out of there and retrieve his laundry. Oh, Howard was one of God's creatures and all that, unique and special and worthy of respect, but Ishmael felt Howard's path to spiritual redemption might be a long one, and on this occasion at least he wasn't offering himself as a guide.

'Thanks for the drink but I'd really better be . . .'

'Oh no you don't. Just you wait here.'

Howard rushed out of the room. He was trembling and sweating. You had to feel sorry for the poor chap. A middle-aged man, living alone, probably his wife had died or had left him, it was bound to make you a bit inward-looking and weird. He was probably just lonely. He shouldn't be ashamed to go to one of those agencies and meet a good woman to keep him company in his autumnal years. Ishmael thought he'd find a way of suggesting this when Howard returned.

In early 1937 Haupt Sturmführer Albert Liese is recruiting members of the SS to form a large team of drivers to test

Dr Porsche's latest prototype, the car now designated the Kraft-durch-Freudewagen. Since the Avus episode, which is known to and envied by his fellow-soldiers, Peter Baldung seems a natural choice. He wants to be part of the process that brings National Socialism to the working man. He also thinks that being a test driver might be fun.

When Howard returned he was wearing a leather dog-collar, a black latex posing pouch and nothing else. It did not seem the best moment to advise him on personal problems.

'You know,' Ishmael started, 'there are many rooms in the mansion of human sexuality but whatever you've got in mind I'd just as soon keep this one locked.'

'I hope you're not going to turn out to be a tease,' Howard said. 'It's very, very simple. I lie on the floor with my face under the glass table. You lower your blue leathers and you defecate on to the glass. That's all, no touching, no sexual contact, no possibility of disease. And you'd make an ageing man very happy.'

Peter is indeed selected, along with perhaps a hundred others. Dr Porsche demonstrates the car to them, and each day they go along to the SS barracks in Kornwestheim, not far from the Porsche villa, and there they collect the motorcars that they will come to know intimately and to despise.

What would Debby have said if she could see her Barry now? Probably she would have sent for an exorcist and the vice squad. Then Ishmael remembered that he had set out on this journey for the sake of new feelings and experiences, and doing what Howard was asking would certainly be a new experience and a half. Howard had been kind with the offer to share a washer, had been free with his gin, and Ishmael was even in need of a bowel movement since the breakfast had worked its way through. But still . . . He dithered.

'Pervy sex outside the context of a meaningful relationship would really be a mockery of the values I hold most dear.'

'Dearie, underneath that cigarette lighter, the one shaped like a boatplane, you'll find four fifty-pound notes. They're yours if you do what I ask. And don't give me any balls about meaningful relationships.'

Peter Baldung's superiors have made it clear that he is not involved in a perk, in some piece of apolitical joyriding. He is taking part in a rigorous scientific experiment, an experiment which seems above all to exist in conditions of nightmarish security.

Peter is not allowed to discuss the tests, not in any way, except with the management and the SS officers involved with the project; and he must swear an oath to this effect, and this oath will not only apply now but for an indefinite period in the future.

He must report any and every observation or incident concerning the car, regardless of how trivial those incidents may appear to him, for he is, after all, not the one to judge. Of course, he is not allowed to take any passenger in the test vehicle, nor must any third party be shown any document or drawing or report or set of results that relate to the vehicle in any way. Smoking and drinking while with the car is naturally forbidden. Photographing the car is not absolutely forbidden, but any film containing an image of the vehicle must be given undeveloped to the management.

The management also retain the right to change any or all of these regulations at any time they see fit, and also to impose any new regulations as and when they seem necessary or desirable. Any breach of the regulations will result in the test driver being instantly reported to the Gestapo.

As Peter Baldung takes his Beetle out for the tenth day of alpine testing he concludes that motoring may not be quite the joy he had always hoped it would be.

An hour later Ishmael was back on the road. He had clean, freshly laundered clothes. He had taken off his blue leathers. He drove to a motor accessory shop and blew most of the two hundred pounds on having bucket seats fitted, and as an extra treat he bought himself a gear knob in the shape of a skull.

Life, Ishmael thought, wasn't so bad.

Three

Yes, Ishmael did sometimes think of Debby in those first few days, and not just when he had laundry to do. The last time he saw her she was giggling in an hysterical way and her last words to him were, 'I knew it. I always knew you were mentally unbalanced, Barry Osgathorpe.'

He had taken her out to see the car. She let out a yelp.

'What the fuck do you call that?' she said.

'Enlightenment.'

They talked about this and that, about where they were going, whether they were going by the same form of transport. Ishmael tried to communicate his thoughts about his new-found need to be himself, but it was water off a duck's back to Debby.

Finally, Ishmael said, 'You see, Debby, there's a party in my head and I'm afraid you're not on the guest list.'

He thought that was a good line.

They were too separate, like two cars heading towards traffic lights – one car gets a filter arrow, the other car gets stuck at a red light. Their paths diverge, they never meet again. Debby was stuck at the traffic lights.

And another reason why he left her was that she'd never give him a good blow job.

Oh, she'd have a bit of a lick, an affectionate nuzzle even, but Ishmael had heard, had read in magazines and in some of the more salacious volumes in the library, about taut purple members plunging relentlessly into scarlet-painted mouths and before you knew where you were there were torrents of hot semen coursing like molten lava down someone's moist, eager, yielding throat. That was the sort of thing he'd had in mind.

You try suggesting that to Debby.

The M62 between Huddersfield and Manchester: it is a ribbon of fitful dreams that scores through the Pennines like the slash of a Stanley knife.

The M1 at the Tinsley Viaduct: it has always provided a view of Hell. It skirts and looks down on the industrial end of Sheffield. To drive along it in the early seventies was to be a spectator at a nightmare vision of steel furnaces, slow-moving white pollution, doorways that farted flame into the sodium-stained darkness.

Today that particular nightmare is over. There is no fire, no steel, no work. The furnaces are exorcized. They are merely sculpture. To an unemployed steel-worker this is a more potent form of nightmare.

The A13 where Ishmael found himself now: a southern road. If you want to travel from East Ham to Shoeburyness it's the road for you. Did Ishmael want to travel from East Ham to Shoeburyness? Well, yes and no. To the Zen motorist all roads are in many ways the same. Yet each road is unique and has its own spirit. Even the A13.

'Somebody should write a song about it,' thought Ishmael.

The A13 is neither town nor country. It is built for cars rather than people. As he drove past the gigantic Ford works at Dagenham Ishmael had a sense of 'this is where it all began'. Henry Ford. History is bunk. The colonization of our fantasies. The production line as dream factory. Henry Ford as Walt Disney.

Ishmael drove past the Circus Tavern and saw that coming attractions included Lulu and Jim Davidson.

He saw people at the roadside selling cut flowers from red plastic buckets. How strange it all seemed.

And then he saw her again – Marilyn. Was it just

coincidence? Is there any such thing?

He was getting petrol. He felt suddenly depressed at seeing the 'Self-Service' signs. They represented so much that was wrong with the world, people serving their self-interests rather than serving some higher order like 'Reality' or 'Truth'. When will they ever learn?

Karl has three great passions in life – the Volkswagen Beetle, although, being an American he calls it a 'Bug', the works of James Joyce, and his girlfriend Cindy.

He loves the Volkswagen in all its many forms – the Kubelwagen, the Schwimmwagen, the Hebmuller; from the Prototype 12 to the historic split-window; from the Reichspost truck to the Karmann-built convertible (one of which he owns). And he even has a soft spot for the Karmann Ghia coupé, sand rails, Volkswagen-based beach buggies, 'Things' and Baja Bugs.

James Joyce represents a more reasoned passion. He has studied *A Portrait of the Artist as a Young Man* in High School, read *Ulysses* with pleasure, and is writing a paper on Joyce for his BA. He often reads *Giacomo Joyce* just for fun, *Finnegans Wake* as a kind of intellectual mud-wrestling, and if he has to spend a night in a motel he makes sure he has the letters with him.

Ishmael filled Enlightenment with three star and was just checking his tyre pressures when a Rolls-Royce pulled on to the forecourt. First an extremely well-to-do couple got out. They were middle aged but tanned and healthy and expensively dressed. Then Marilyn got out. Her clothes were the same as she had been wearing two days ago, but he was right, she had been wearing a wig. This was now gone. She was still blonde but less violently so. From Beetle to Rolls-Royce, some would say this was a step-up in the world. Ishmael hoped she wasn't still tearing her clothes and demanding money.

The couple put petrol in their car and Marilyn went to the Ladies. Ishmael thought about going over and chatting but he didn't want to intrude. The couple seemed to be watching Marilyn very closely.

Ishmael finished checking his tyres, got into his car and decided to leave Marilyn to her new associates, to let her live in her own space.

In his mirror he saw her returning from the Ladies. She went briskly over to the Rolls-Royce, leaned inside, snatched the car keys and started running. The man made a grab for her but she swerved away from him and flung his keys hard and high into the middle of the A13. The man wasn't sure whether to pursue the keys or Marilyn. He went for the keys while his wife chased Marilyn. Ishmael wondered whether he should go over to smooth things out. However, Marilyn was now running straight for Enlightenment. She gave one of her screams.

'Start your car. Get me out of here.'

Instinct took over. Another human being was reaching out to him. He started the engine, revved hard and threw open the passenger door. Marilyn had a ten-yard lead on the woman. She made it easily. They burned off along the A13 with a satisfying squeal of rubber.

The woman was standing on the forecourt yelling in a very cultured voice, 'Marilyn, Marilyn, come back here. Come back here at once. Your father and I are very upset.'

Ishmael's suspicions were aroused.

The man was trying to stop the traffic to retrieve his keys. On the A13 this was quite an ambitious project. When Ishmael eventually lost sight of him he was standing in the middle of the road attempting to stop the cars but only succeeding in getting a lot of abuse from drivers as they narrowly missed him.

Karl likes Cindy too. They meet at the University of Santa Barbara at Isla Vista. Cindy is acting in the *Jew of*

Malta. Karl is doing box office. He watches every performance (there are three), and on the last night he falls in love with her. This is convenient. They 'get together' at the cast party and never look back.

Marilyn sat in the passenger seat. She was panting.

'New seats,' she said.

'They recline.'

Without the wig she looked different, much younger. She wasn't wearing much make-up either. She had a clear complexion. She looked something of an English rose.

'What was going on back there?' Ishmael asked. 'Only if you want to tell me, that is.'

She seemed very hesitant. At last she reached inside her jacket.

'You ought to have this back,' she said.

She pulled twenty-five pounds from a very fat roll of notes.

'You didn't rob those people, did you?' Ishmael asked.

'No, no, they gave it to me.'

Her voice too was different. It was gentler, more refined, posher.

'Why did they do that?'

'Just parental affection, I suppose.'

Things were getting tangled.

'They're my parents,' she said. 'The money, the Rolls-Royce, that's what my background is really like. I was lying to you. I was just acting. I only told you that story to get money out of you.'

'But you didn't need it.'

'A paradox, eh?'

'Don't tell me,' Ishmael said. 'It's the old story – rich parents who give you everything except love. So you ran away. Understandable enough. And they chase after you trying to recapture you and put you back in the padded, opulent cage of their making. That's it, isn't it?'

39

'Well, sort of.'

Ishmael nodded. He had a feeling for these things.

'Actually,' she said, 'I'm doing research for my first novel.'

They passed a road sign that said Shoeburyness was twenty-four miles away.

'My parents want me to go back to Oxford and finish my degree. *I* want to be free.'

This was what Ishmael had journeyed so far to hear.

Karl and Cindy spend the summer making love, reading Joyce aloud and touring in Karl's Beetle convertible. He has the car resprayed in red metalflake with some very tasteful black pinstriping. He has to take out another student loan to pay for it all but he considers it worthwhile. He has fitted a zoom tube, a set of moon discs, and a pair of baby turbo mirrors. They drive out to the edge of the desert, read *Pomes Penyeach*, and fuck naked amid the scrub and sand.

Marilyn, it appeared, was working on a novel about a girl who is studying Philosophy, Politics and Economics at Oxford University, but really the girl wants to write a novel. However, she feels she has no experience of life so she takes to the road, hitches, screws around, gets drunk, gets molested, gets tattooed, gets chased around the country by her parents, and meets lots of fascinating and colourful characters, including the man of her dreams. They buy some land, become self-sufficient, she writes a bestseller, and they have half a dozen gifted children.

Ishmael thought it sounded like a good read.

'And am I one of the fascinating and colourful characters?' he asked.

'I'll say.'

'Where's your tattoo?'

'I'll show you when we get to a motel.'

'Motel?'

'Yes, I thought we should go to a motel and have raunchy sex in the middle of the afternoon.'

Ishmael narrowly kept control of the wheel.

But graduation is coming, job recruitment threatens, and student love often dies in a last minute dash for good grades. Karl and Cindy see less of each other in these crucial weeks though that is his decision not hers. Karl completes his paper on the 'difficulty' of Joyce's parody in *Ulysses* and this absorbs him to such an extent that he can't even find time to replace the dying starter motor in his car. And Cindy, loving Karl more than ever, feels lonely, resentful, and resigns herself to a so-so degree in Communications.

Then Karl gets the news that he has won the Xavier Clinton Harley scholarship in James Joyce studies and the chance to visit the University of Texas and spend six months with Joyce manuscripts.

'It's too good an offer to turn down,' he tells Cindy. 'And after all, six months is no time at all. We'll write. I'll call you. Nothing need have changed when I get back.'

Cindy wonders whether he is trying to deceive her or himself.

'Yes,' she says. 'Everything will be fine when you get back. I'll make sure of that.'

The A13 is not a Mecca for cheap, sordid motels. In fact, the only one Ishmael knew was just outside Cambridge. It was a long drive but they were free spirits with all the time in the world. What's a couple of hours and a few gallons of petrol when you have all eternity in front of you?

And of course they had so much to discuss. Ishmael had never met a student of philosophy before. Mostly she talked and he listened. There were more things in her philosophy than Ishmael had ever dreamed of. They chatted about Spinoza, Russell, Kant and Bergson. They chewed the fat over Existentialism, Egoism and Platonism. Marilyn tried him out with a few old chestnuts like the self and others, appearance and reality, free will and predestination. It was heady stuff.

'Imagine an island,' she said.

'I might have heard this one before.'

'The inhabitants are all female and are either virgins or nymphomaniacs. The virgins always lie. The nymphomaniacs always tell the truth. Now, if you met an inhabitant from the island, what question would you ask her in order to determine whether she was a virgin or a nymphomaniac?'

'I give up,' Ishmael said.

'You wouldn't need to ask any questions,' Marilyn said. 'You can always spot a nymphomaniac. It's something about the eyes.'

She explained this was her little joke. Ishmael was finding this whole philosophy business a lot more tricky than he had imagined. He was more at home with a few simple concepts.

'But philosophy is not about a few simple concepts,' Marilyn said.

'Oh come on,' said Ishmael, 'it is to me. I may not know much about metaphysics but I know what I like. A tank full of petrol, a head full of relevation, that's *my* philosophy and I'm sticking to it.'

'You know,' Marilyn said, 'this attitude you have towards cars is really profoundly working class, if you don't mind my saying so.'

Ishmael did mind. That hurt. The Zen motorist likes to think of himself as classless. He would have to think that one through.

Six months is plenty of time for some scars to heal, not enough for others. Cindy is determined to remain one of Karl's passions.

The months pass. Joycean letters cross the States, and finally Cindy gets a letter that says Karl will be home 'at the end of the month'. Cindy is hurt by the lack of precision, and Karl's letter says that he will have one or two things to sort out before he sees her, things like getting the Bug out of storage, seeing what needs doing to it.

Karl does indeed come home at the end of the month but it is well into the next month before he makes contact with Cindy. He is warm on the phone and says he'll be round at about six, they'll go for a drive.

'How's the Bug?' Cindy asks.

'Bugs don't change much,' he says and chuckles.

Ishmael discovered that it is a legal requirement to give your name and address when registering at a motel. He wrote 'Ishmael, c/o The Road', but that didn't go down too well. In the end he wrote 'Mr and Mrs Smith'. It was just like the movies.

Another requirement, at least in this case, was payment in advance. The receptionist looked at Ishmael and Marilyn, looked at the car, and then insisted.

Their only luggage was Marilyn's shoulder-bag, and a large brown paper bag containing Ishmael's leather suit. He never knew when it might come in handy. When they got to their room Marilyn took a bottle of champagne and a side of smoked salmon out of her bag. They sat on the edge of the bed and drank from the bottle.

'This is good champagne,' Ishmael said, though he wasn't sure it was.

'I only shoplift the best,' Marilyn replied.

They took off their clothes and got into bed.

To cut a long story short, Marilyn's tattoo was on her buttock and it was of a snake. They made love. Ishmael offered the opinion that it was transcendent though he didn't have much to compare it with, only Debby and a girl called Eunice whom he'd met very briefly at a party.

'What's your favourite position?' he asked.

'Foetal,' Marilyn replied.

She explained that was another joke. Ishmael suddenly thought he should have brought his vibrator and attachments in from the car.

At five o'clock Karl rings the bell to Cindy's apartment. She isn't ready for him but his earliness seems like a good sign. She quickly puts on old jeans and a sweatshirt and runs down to the front door of the apartment building to greet him on the doorstep. They kiss. It is passionate enough.

'Come in,' she says.

'Nah,' says Karl. 'Let's go for a drive.'

'Where's the car?' she asks, looking up and down the street.

'There.'

Marilyn got out of bed to have a shower. Ishmael was dozing and thinking higher thoughts when he heard the gentle crunch of metal from outside. He got up and looked out of the window. Someone had run their car into a bollard in the car-park. It was a Rolls-Royce. It was Marilyn's parents' car. Enlightenment was clearly visible in front of Reception. Mother and father got out. They looked at the damaged rear wing, shouted at each other accusingly and strode into the lobby of the motel.

There was nothing else for it. There are times when a man does not run. He was going to have to reason with them. He put on his blue leathers. He stuck his head into the bathroom and told Marilyn he was popping out for some fresh air.

Karl points to a white 1968 Corvette parked at the corner of the block.

'Why?' Cindy asks.

'Well,' says Karl, he has obviously been rehearsing this. 'When you're out in Texas, in that big country, a Volkswagen Bug seems just kinda small, inadequate, like a toy, immature almost. There isn't the power, the acceleration, the handling. I wanted something more. You'll love the Corvette, I know you will. That's what I've been doing these last few days since I got home. I had to trade-in the Bug, had to arrange another loan.'

Ishmael ran to his car, got out the claw hammer, and waited. Marilyn's parents caught sight of him through the glass doors of the motel lobby and came hurrying out. Father arrived first, winning by a couple of lengths.

'Where is she?' he bawled.

'Who?'

'My daughter, who do you bloody well think?'

Ishmael smiled in what he took to be a wry manner.

'You mean the motel wouldn't tell you?'

'As a matter of fact they wouldn't.'

'Marilyn's in one of the rooms,' Ishmael said. 'But there are a lot of rooms.'

'He's got a love bite on his neck.'

It was the mother who said this. She seemed outraged. Ishmael hadn't been aware of the bite until now and was suddenly filled with pride.

'Did Marilyn do that?' the mother demanded.

'Who else? How many women do you think I had in there?'

She nearly smiled at that.

'Don't talk filth in front of me,' the father said.

'I'll talk filth in front of anybody I like,' said Ishmael. 'Piles, urethra, prepuce, labia minor!'

The father was sweating freely. So for that matter was Ishmael, but on hearing this 'filth' Marilyn's father's face turned startlingly red and he screamed, 'If you're looking for trouble young man, you've found trouble.'

He stripped off his jacket, tossed it to the ground with a flourish and started to roll up his sleeves. Ishmael took a step forward, lazily raised the claw hammer and swept it in an accelerating arc that made contact with one of the newly bared elbows. Marilyn's father let out a cry that was part pain and part disbelief, and he paced exaggeratedly in a circle flapping the injured arm.

'I'll sue for that,' he said.

Ishmael laughed.

'To live outside the law you must be honest,' he cajoled. 'I'm not looking for trouble, that's the very last thing I'm looking for. There are a million things I want to find, but trouble isn't one of them. I want to find an army with the motto "Yield". I want to find a timetable that obeys a body clock. I want to find a roundabout called stillness. I want to find a milkman who doesn't know how to whistle. I want to find me and I wouldn't mind finding you. I want to find a bypass on the ring road to oblivion. I never knew that I wanted to find Marilyn but now that I have found her I realize that I was looking for her all along. I want to find the still point in the turning circle. I want to find a Messiah who doesn't believe his own press releases.'

He could have gone on. He was feeling quite inspired.

'This boy is raving,' the father said.

Ishmael said, 'Your daughter isn't running away. She's running towards something – towards herself. The lay-by cannot stop the accelerating lane from joining the motorway. You cannot stop Marilyn. You can only bid her *bon voyage*, wish her a pleasant journey and hope that she arrives at her chosen destination.'

The mother moved with grace and speed, pulled the hammer away from Ishmael and before he could react she had smashed both of Enlightenment's headlights. A tyre blew out in his head. He was mad. He grabbed the woman by the throat and forced her to the ground, but as they hit the tarmac the father was on him. The three of them wrestled around for a while. Ishmael received a hammer blow in the groin. The woman was deadly with that thing. Meanwhile the father had Ishmael's head gripped firmly in both hands and was banging it against the Beetle's rear nearside wing. One or other would lose its shape.

Ishmael, never the street-fighter, was now dragged to his feet. He stood, or rather was held in front of Enlightenment. A stylish upper-cut threw him back on to the car's bonnet. Tiny neon strips in gold and red burst behind his eyes. They looked pretty enough. He slowly slid down the slope of the car while being kicked regularly, accurately and with enormous passion.

He would certainly have taken a lot more punishment if Marilyn's voice had not then said, 'Leave him alone. It's me you want.'

The father was fighting mad. He put an armlock on his daughter.

'Run away, Marilyn,' Ishmael shouted. 'Save yourself.'

But it appeared Marilyn did not want to be saved. She didn't struggle. She allowed herself to be bundled into the Rolls-Royce. All Ishmael could do was keep still. The pain was less that way. As a parting shot the mother threw the hammer at him. It missed but took a hefty chunk out of the Beetle's paintwork. The Rolls drove away.

Cindy sobs, slams the front door of the building and runs back to her own apartment. Karl leans on the bell for a long time but eventually stops. Cindy hears the loud engine and the Cherry Bomb exhaust as he drives away.

Ishmael was down. His leathers were scratched. The Rolls

was out of view. There was no longer any hurry to go anywhere.

But as he lay there he became aware of a jacket on the tarmac, not very far away. It was, of course, the jacket that Marilyn's father had taken off and thrown down. Ishmael reached for it. There was a wallet in the inside pocket. It contained a photograph of Marilyn, perhaps a hundred pounds in cash, a gold American Express card, and a driving licence that gave Marilyn's father's name, age and home address.

Ishmael had smashed headlamps to replace. After that it was simple. He had to rescue a philosophy student in distress.

Cindy stops crying in the end. She stands in the centre of her bedroom, in front of the wardrobe mirror, and takes off her clothes. She looks at the reflection of her naked body – not so very naked. Over the last six months she has had tattooed over her back and buttocks a solemn, livid, motorcade of the Volkswagen in all its many forms – the Kubelwagen, the Schwimmwagen, the Hebmuller, the Prototype 12, the historic split-window, the Reichspost truck, the convertible, the Karmann Ghia coupé, sand rails, beach buggies, and Baja Bugs.

Karl's passion for James Joyce remains undiminished.

Four

War? What is it good for? Absolutely nothing. Say it again. At least that's the way it seemed to Ishmael. How did clean-living Barry Osgathorpe come to be involved in a vulgar roadside brawl? There are no easy answers.

He was picking bits of glass out of the broken headlights when a man with very long hair came over to him. The man looked convincingly like a hippy but he was wearing overalls with the motel's logo on them, and had the air of a gardener or maintenance man.

'You OK, man?' he asked Ishmael.

'Bloody great.'

'What was going on there?'

Ishmael didn't answer.

'I'd have helped you, man, but you know violence isn't the answer.'

Ishmael suggested he stop being ridiculous.

'Hey, really, people have got to start loving each other.'

'Oh, sod off,' said Ishmael.

And then he heard himself being negative and hostile and he knew he was wrong.

'In my heart of hearts I know you're right,' he said. 'But do you really expect me to love those two after they smash my car and steal my girl?'

'Well, I'm an idealist,' the hippy said. 'No one ever said it was going to be easy. And you know, "*my* car", "*my* girl" – dubious concepts. Look, I'm just finishing my shift. I don't know if you're heading my way, but maybe you could give me a lift to where I live. It's just up

49

the road at Fox's Farm. It's sort of a commune. You could come over and I could roll us a fat number.'

His simple philosophy had touched Ishmael deeply.

'I'd love to come,' he said, 'but just at the moment I'm on a quest.'

'That sounds great, but you know it's getting late, and it's getting dark, and it doesn't look as though you've got any headlights.'

All this was true.

'My name's John.'

'Call me Ishmael.'

'You'll like Fox's Farm. It's very mellow. We can have some free-range eggs.'

Ishmael thought. Now admittedly he had already paid for a night at the motel, admittedly the most noble thing would have been to pursue Marilyn and her mother and father immediately and to the end of the earth. On the other hand, motels are soulless places and in any case he doubted whether he was all that welcome following the brawl; equally he had Marilyn's address, and her parents weren't going to move house before tomorrow; *and* it was getting late and dark and he didn't have any headlights.

'If you don't like eggs there are always frozen pizzas in the freezer.'

Ah well, Ishmael thought, another adventure. That's what I'm here for. Isn't that what we're all here for?

'Take me to your commune,' he quipped.

Ishmael used to say to Debby, 'Mark but this pig, and mark in this, how little that which thou denies me is.' Since this was obscure he would then say, 'Look, Debby, there are women in this world who are prepared to put their tongues up horses' anuses, who get penetrated by mastiffs, who get their faces doused in pig semen. So frankly, my love, I don't think I'm being entirely unreasonable merely by asking, and very politely at that, if I might gently come in your mouth.'

Frankly, Debby thought he *was* being entirely unreasonable.

'Go find yourself a pig!' she'd say. 'Let your pig do your laundry. You men are all the same.'

Ishmael had never thought that Debby was sufficiently worldly-wise to make that kind of generalization.

'You'd put your penis in my mouth,' she'd continue. 'You'd put it in a pig, you'd put it in half a pound of pork dripping if it didn't answer back.'

Enthusiastic though she was, Marilyn hadn't proved to be an enthusiast for the kind of thing he had in mind, either.

She had sprawled, provocatively enough, on the motel bed and inquired, 'What do you like having done?'

Ishmael replied, 'I like to see torrents of hot semen coursing like molten lava down your moist, eager, yielding throat.'

He laughed coyly.

'Sorry', Marilyn said. 'I'd really have to quite like you before I did that.'

Ishmael thought it best to let the matter drop. But a commune? Surely this was a good location for the aspiring oralist, with its understood promises of self-sufficiency, casual drug-abuse and free love. It might be all slightly old-fashioned, but Ishmael didn't want to knock it until he'd tried it.

He and John the Hippy drove ten miles or so in the gathering dusk. On the way Ishmael told his story. John the Hippy seemed impressed. They drove down ever more minor roads until they came to a track that ran through a scrubby bit of woodland. A building was visible. It was a modern, sprawling bungalow with a distinct touch of the commuter-belt about it. Doors and windowframes had, however, been painted in what might still be called psychedelic colours. There was a number of outbuildings – a double garage, a couple of sheds, a disused stable – and scattered among them were the wrecks of old cars, motorcycles, minibuses and caravanettes. Ishmael didn't take to the place.

The little girl who peered through the Benz showroom window with Peter, who had her ears boxed by Adolf Hitler, is called Nina. Half Austrian, half Swiss she grows up with ambitions to become an actress. She cannot decide whether she would be happier as a serious Brechtian ensemble player or as a Hollywood sex symbol, Hollywood having been forced to develop a taste for things and people European these recent years.

She practises giving interviews. The Hollywood option seems to trip more easily from her tongue. 'I have a love affair with the camera,' she explains, 'and my career would always come before any man.'

August 1938 finds her still in Berlin. Bertolt Brecht is long gone and Nina is singing French, English and German songs in a Troika just off the Tauentzienstrasse, and supplementing her income with a little light-weight prostitution. It is the old story. It's a living.

After her act she mixes with the spare audience. Favours to none, to all she smiles extends, and at the end of the evening she is sharing a table with Richard Huntingdon, an Englishman, sometime journalist, sometime poet, sometime luster after a man in a uniform.

'We have special cause for celebration tonight,' Nina says.

'Why is that?'

She shows him her Kunst-der-Freude-Wagen-Sparkarte – her Volkswagen saver's card.

'Nice place you have here,' Ishmael lied.

'We like it,' said John the Hippy.

Ishmael parked the car. They got out.

'No need to lock the car,' Ishmael said brightly, thinking that a commune would surely be the one place guaranteed not to rip-off a traveller.

'Oh, I don't know,' said John the Hippy. 'You can't be too careful these days.'

Yes, thought Ishmael, the sixties ended a long time ago.

Nudity, wholefood, group sex, arts and crafts, lots of very small children with names like Mothership, loud rock music, a lot of personal and political commitment, and a general refusal to work on Maggie's Farm – these were the things that Ishmael had expected from your standard commune.

The reality was somewhat different. Ishmael discovered with horror that several of the men were wearing ties. They had day-jobs where they had to dress up like 'straights' but even when they got back to the commune they kept the 'straight' clothes on. OK, so the girl who was cooking supper for everybody had a gold stud through her nose, but when the meal was served there didn't appear to be anything very, say, macrobiotic about it. It was pie and chips. No slap in the face for the bourgeoisie there.

Richard takes the saver's card and examines it carefully. He sees the Gothic print and seemingly endless spaces for the sticking of savings stamps.

'I am to be the owner of one of Herr Hitler's Strength-Through-Joy cars,' she says giggling. 'The people's car.'

'Smashing,' says Richard. 'Congratulations. When are you taking me for a ride in it?'

'Oh, the moment it's delivered, I promise you.'

'Is there much of a wait? A few weeks? A month?'

'Richard,' she says in mock anger, 'don't be so naive. Obviously the car isn't delivered until it's paid for.'

'I'm not sure I follow.'

'It's very simple. I save five Marks each week . . .'

'How much does this car cost?'

'Nine hundred and ninety Marks.'

Richard winces.

'I simply save five Marks every week, a stamp is put on the card, and when the card is full, and when the cars are in full production, I shall have one.'

The only stereotype about communes that Fox's Farm helped to reinforce was that everyone seemed drugged, positively sedated. He saw perhaps a dozen inmates, there was no way of telling what relationship anyone had with anyone else, no way of telling what they were, what they felt, not even what their names were. And the main reason for this was that nobody ever said anything. Nobody asked him to sit down, nobody introduced themselves. They didn't seem to notice him. They just sat around eating, drinking and being sullen.

Ishmael was against meaningless chatter as much as the next man, but he had to start somewhere. He tried to make conversation.

'Nice lifestyle you have here,' he said, though his heart was not in the remark and perhaps they were aware of it since they completely ignored it.

Perhaps they were inhibited because he was a stranger, so what better way of overcoming this than by avoiding social niceties completely and getting right down to brass tacks.

'Look, what's your ideology here?' he asked.

The intense silence around the table became, if possible, even more profound, but he did seem to have provoked some reaction. The woman with the nose-stud looked up from her meal and stared out of the window, her eyes fixed on some distant object invisible to the naked eye.

'We talk about ideology,' she said. 'We talk as though we know who we are and where we're going; but we're lost. Most of us are very, very lost.'

'I once was lost, but now I'm found,' Ishmael said.

This did produce a vague mutter from one or two of the people around the table, but Ishmael couldn't tell if this indicated approval.

'But will take four years,' Richard says, aghast.

'Yes. It's a long-term plan. You're always telling me that I should not live so much in the present. I thought about it for a long time. Besides, there will be hundreds of thousands of us all saving together through this marvellous scheme.'

'Hundreds of thousands of you, each paying five Marks a week for a car that you will not see for at the very least four years? It sounds as though some of you Germans have more money than sense.'

'You think the German people are unwise?'

'Let's just say I don't see the English workman falling for this inverted form of usury.'

Lightening the mood Ishmael asked, 'Does anybody know where there's a good cheap Volkswagen garage around here?'

A man in a tie said that he did, and he gave the impression that given time he might even tell where it was.

Then the meal was over. Everybody stood up and went into the living-room to watch television and take some drugs. Ishmael felt unwanted and unwelcome. He went to look again at the damage done to Enlightenment. He stood drinking in the night air and picking flakes of paint off the driver's door.

A few minutes later the man who knew where the Volkswagen garage was came out. He handed Ishmael a slip of paper with an address and a map on it. Ishmael got the feeling that this was to be considered a grand gesture and thanked him accordingly. The tie-wearer nodded and left.

Then John the Hippy came out.

'That was beautiful,' he said. 'Just beautiful.'

'Huh?'

'The way you talked at supper. It was so precise, so intense. We don't believe in pointless talk. We believe in clearing the mind of babble, and it's obvious you feel the same way. You're only concerned with fundamentals – lifestyle, ideology, how to get your Volkswagen repaired, the nitty-gritty.'

Ishmael hadn't even been trying.

'We think you're a very wise man. We think you're something special. We wondered if you might stay here for a while, be a kind of spiritual guide.'

This seemed a bit extreme, even to Ishmael.

'I'm flattered of course, but there are other places I have to be.'

'Shit, it's always the same with gurus. Where do you have to be?'

'Wherever Marilyn is. I thought I'd talk to her father. It won't be easy, but I think the direct approach is usually best. I thought I'd ask for his daughter's hand, something like that.'

'Wow.'

'All right, so he and his wife beat me up, but at least we were communicating. It was very brief but I did detect a glimmer of genuine contact, and that makes me believe that I can reach out to him as one human being to another.'

'You certainly cut through the bullshit,' John the Hippy said. 'You're a lesson to us all. You get beaten up, your car gets vandalized, you lose your girl yet you keep your wisdom.'

'What else have I got? What else has anybody got, John?'

John the Hippy was speechless.

'Thank you,' he said.

'Here,' said Ishmael, 'I'd like you to have this.'

He reached into his pocket and produced the Gold American Express card that had belonged to Marilyn's father.

'Take it,' Ishmael continued. 'I think the owner may be too preoccupied for the time being to get round to reporting it missing. You can probably get a couple of days' use out of it.'

John the Hippy beamed.

Then one of the girls came from the bungalow. She was in her early teens, had silky hair, shorts and a personal stereo.

'And *we'd* like you to have *this*,' she said.

She handed Ishmael a grubby envelope. Inside were two squares of blotting paper, each with a small, dark stain at its centre.

'Acid,' she said. 'The American Express card of the mind.'

'We all know about your English workman,' Nina says. 'Besides, he has never been fortunate enough to have the opportunity of buying such a special vehicle. Cheap to run, cheap to service, whatever that means, designed by Dr Porsche, you know. Herr Hitler has already laid the foundation stone of a huge factory for the car. He has begun building autobahnen. In four years you will envy me.'

'If, in four years, you have seen so much as one rubber tyre, I shall indeed be very surprised.'

'But already the cars are being driven, admittedly only by leading members of the Nazi Party at this stage, but . . .'

'If you want my opinion, they are the only people ever likely to drive them.'

'I'm not sure that I do want your opinion. It depresses me. I prefer to think that the German economic recovery will continue, that it will accelerate, bringing greater prosperity for all, and then I may have my Volkswagen in much less than four years.'

Next morning Ishmael drove the couple of miles to the address he had been given for the Volkswagen garage. It was down a dry mud track that ran between a row of blackened railway arches and a set of allotments. At first there was just a mass of tall weeds and a few derelict bits of motorcar that were recognizably from Beetles. Then, poking above the weeds were four complete cars parked in a neat line, and a little way off a pale blue Beetle in front of a door that opened into one of the arches. Above the door was a hand-painted sign that read 'Fat Les – the Vee-Dub King'. There was nobody visible but the music of Wagner, played at awesome volume, came from inside the arch. The door was open a couple of feet. Ishmael stuck his head inside. The music grew louder but he couldn't see anyone. It was dark. He entered and trod on half a hamburger. Then he detected a movement in a dark corner and saw a rather fat, sweaty, unshaven forty-year-old man, Les he supposed, sitting up in a tartan sleeping-bag.

'Good morning,' Ishmael shouted politely above the music.

Fat Les seemed half asleep or still half drunk, or both. He waved a weary hand at Ishmael.

'Sorry, Wagner old mate,' he said, and reached out a hand to turn off the music. 'That's my get up and go music. Doesn't always work. I suppose you've got a Volkswagen.'

'I certainly have,' Ishmael said proudly.

Fat Les got out of his sleeping-bag. He was naked but for a pair of nylon, paisley briefs.

'I suppose it needs something doing to it.'

'Yes. I need some new headlights.'

That didn't seem to make Fat Les very happy. He shambled around the garage for a while, pulled on a shirt, picked up a few cold chips from a paper plate, searched half-heartedly for trousers, looked at Ishmael accusingly.

'And if your Herr Hitler plunges Europe into war?'

'Then, Herr Richard, I suppose it will not much matter if we have our own motorcars or not.'

'Then *I* suppose, Nina, your fine motor factory, dedicated to producing cars for the people, might very easily be switched to military production, and who knows, your people's car itself could perhaps quite easily be converted into a vehicle of war.'

'Did you see my sign outside?'

'Oh yes,' said Ishmael.

'Remember what it said?'

'Fat Les – the Vee-Dub King.'

'Right. The King. Not Fat Les the Vee-Dub bodger, not Fat Les the Vee-Dub wanker. The King.'

'It's a very nice sign. Did you do it yourself?'

Fat Les stared at him, as sullen as a hippy from Fox's Farm.

'Let me tell you something.'

'Please,' said Ishmael.

'Let me tell you what I do with Volkswagens.'

'This is really great.'

'Let's say you need a new engine. You could have it rebored, turboed, hot-rodded, supercharged. I could bolt in a Porsche, or we could get really flash and put a Rover V8 up the front end. Then we'd get new carbs, heavy-duty fan and oil cooler, racing cam, performance exhaust, probably with a zoom tube. If we're doing that lot you're going to have to up-rate your suspension and your brakes, and put in an anti-roll bar, and you'd be daft not to do something with your wheels – slot mags, dish mags, alloys, low profiles, 135 fronts, 165 rears. I can chop it for you, channel it for you, section it, french it, louvre it, raise it or lower it, front or back. I can nose and deck it. I can give you spoilers, fins, whale tails, portholes. No problem. If you want to get really technical I can put in a cocktail cabinet in the back seat that plays "Born to Run" every time you open it.'

'Great,' said Ishmael.

'But you just want a new set of headlights.'

'Yes please,' said Ishmael.

He was very impressed by Fat Les. Of course, he hadn't understood more than a few words that his speech had contained but it was so refreshing to meet someone so clearly involved and in love with his work.

Fat Les was sullen again. There was a long silence.

'Just a pair of headlights,' Ishmael said again brightly. 'That's all today, thank you.'

He laughed nervously. The silence continued.

'I suppose I'd better have a look at this motor of yours then,' Fat Les said at last.

He never did find his trousers. He walked out in his shirt and briefs and looked at Enlightenment. He gave a deep, a cosmic sigh and circled the Beetle. He looked at it from all angles, sometimes getting down on the ground and poking the chassis with his fingers, causing little showers of rust. As he continued the inspection his spirits plummeted, and by the time he'd finished it was as though he had been plunged into a well of weariness and despair. He looked at Ishmael, who was too frightened to say anything.

'Yes, you do need new headlights.'

Ishmael nodded eagerly. He thought of telling Fat Les

the whole story of how they had come to be smashed but Fat Les was not looking receptive.

'You also need new tyres, new brake pipes and cylinders, new sills, about three hundred pounds of welding . . .'

He went on like this for a while. Ishmael tried to pretend that he knew what Fat Les was talking about.

'Let's face it, old son, you need a new car.'

'No,' Ishmael said very firmly. 'This car is my vehicle. This car and I go to the end of the road together. You know, sometimes as I drive along with the wind in my hair, because of the hole in the roof, an empty road, the English countryside, the car struggling to get to sixty miles an hour, everything rattling and sounding as though it's about to fall apart, well you might find this silly, but at times like that, this car and I feel like one.'

Fat Les was silent for a very long time. He looked at Ishmael, looked at Enlightenment, at his own car, at the ground, at the sky. He scratched his gut and said, 'I don't think that's silly at all. In fact that's about the most intelligent remark I've heard from a punter in years. Most of the people I have to deal with – they're turds, tossers – they don't care what anybody does to their cars so long as it's cheap and fast. Philistines. No sense. No soul. You, though, I reckon you're all right.'

Fat Les had a pair of headlights in stock and he fitted them on Enlightenment.

'At least your headlights are legal,' he said when he'd finished. 'I wish I could say the same for the rest of it. I just hope the bogies don't stop you.'

'Bogies?'

'Police.'

'Yes, it's so hard to live a life untrammelled by petty restrictions.'

'I'll say. And your car does make you a bit of a target. The fuzz want everybody driving around in neat little boxes, safe little family saloons with as much character as a parking ticket.'

'Ah, Richard,' says Nina wistfully, 'you are too intellectual, too political for me. Allow me my dreams of freedom, of speed and escape.'

'I will allow you anything, my dear, but there are others . . .'

'Then order me another bottle of vintage champagne.'

On the dance floor boys in blazers and girls with cropped hair dance, perform a dumb-show of pleasure. It is no more authentic than the bottle of 'vintage' champagne that is brought to the Englishman's table, no more real than Nina's dream of owning her own car. But in Berlin on that autumn night as goose-steps echo back and forth between the ornate, peeling stucco of tall, terraced houses, as triangles are daubed on front doors, and as shops' windows and faces get smashed, it is all any of them have got.

'I don't want to be safe,' said Ishmael.

'Good for you. On the other hand, if your master cylinder goes while you're braking to avoid a pile-up . . .'

'I suppose there's safety and safety.'

'I suppose there is.'

'I've decided it's time to take a few risks.'

'I can see that,' Fat Les said looking at Enlightenment. 'How far do you have to get exactly?'

So of course Ishmael had to tell him the whole story. Fat Les was a great listener.

'So you're just going to *talk* to her father?'

'Initially, yes.'

'And when that doesn't work?'

'Well I abhor violence. Something will come to me.'

'I hope it's the kind of something that gets him in the goolies before he gets you.'

'I'll keep it in mind,' Ishmael said. 'But I still believe in the value of one human being talking to another.'

'But does her father?'

'I think I can make him see things my way.'

'You're a weird bugger, aren't you?'

'I've heard people say that sort of thing.'

He'd heard people like Debby, Marilyn, Marilyn's mother and father, the people who used to work with him in the library, the man in the yellow cardigan, Howard with the rattan table, though who was he to talk?

Fat Les went over to his own Beetle and ran his hand over the roof. The hand was short, fat and oil-stained, but it was a loving hand.

'This Beetle of mine has a top speed of a hundred and twenty miles per hour, nought to sixty in seven seconds,' Fat Les said. 'If the fuzz ever chased me, and if they ever caught me, which they couldn't, they'd still never believe that the car was capable of the sort of speeds I do in it. That's the advantage of going like a million dollars and looking like forty-five quid.'

'Appearance and reality,' said Ishmael.

'Your car looks like a ten-bob postal order that's gone past its expiry date.'

Ishmael shrugged.

Fat Les pointed at the row of four Beetles.

'I don't suppose you'd consider borrowing one of them, would you?'

'No,' said Ishmael.

'I didn't suppose you would.'

'There are certain journeys that must be made in certain ways,' Ishmael said.

'Yeah,' said Fat Les. 'I reckon you're not wrong.'

'How much for the headlights?' asked Ishmael.

'No charge.'

'Come on, we road warriors like to pay our way.'

'No, you're the most entertainment I've had in this place in a decade.'

63

Ishmael started Enlightenment. He was setting off to perform a desperate act of rescue. He hoped he was man enough. He thought he probably was, just about, on a good day.

'Just one thing,' Les shouted above the grind of the engine. 'If talking doesn't work, and if by any chance you get involved in a bit of aggro, and if you're in a position to do it; give the bastard one for me.'

Five

And so it was that Ishmael continued his odyssey of crazy mixed-up youth, getting nowhere fast; racing across the heartland of England to wherever life is lived fastest, on a road that must be taken in top gear, foot flat to the floor, feeding his hunger for sensation; sensation at any price. It was better than working in a library.

And then he saw a hitch-hiker. He was young and male, about seventeen, skinny, failing to grow a moustache. Ishmael didn't want to give anyone a lift. When you're on a quest-cum-mercy-errand you really don't want to be bothered with the dreary conversations you have with most hitch-hikers. Then he felt he was being uncharitable. The hitch-hiker started waving his arms wildly. Ishmael vaguely recognized him. Then the hitch-hiker jumped into the road in front of the car. This was madness but perhaps he was more trusting of Enlightenment's brakes than he had any reason to be. Some time later, some distance away, having swerved to avoid running him down, Ishmael stopped the car. The hitch-hiker came running.

'Ishmael,' he shouted. 'It's me.'

He looked familiar. Ishmael noticed the studded leather jacket, the ghetto-blaster, the hands that, for all he knew, were deadly weapons.

'Davey, isn't it?'

'You remembered.'

Ishmael nodded.

'You'd better get in,' he said. 'But I warn you, I'm on a

quest-cum-mercy-errand and I don't want to be bothered with the dreary conversations you have with most hitch-hikers.'

'Me neither, Ishmael. I've only got time for the really big issues.'

'Really?'

'Sure. You changed my life. I've been looking for you since you left the motorway services. Amazing stroke of luck to find you again. I've been hitching all over the place for the last couple of days. I turned down loads of lifts. But I knew that if I needed to find you, I would.'

'Really?'

'Sure. Really Zen, eh?'

'Why did you need to find me?'

'Because you changed my life. I could have spent the rest of my life playing computer games, doing martial-arts classes. What a waste of potential. You made me see it was a phase, a bad phase. I'm ready to move on to the *next* phase.'

'That's terrific,' Ishmael said. 'What's the next phase going to be?'

'I thought you'd tell me.'

'Ah.'

'I felt sure you'd know what I ought to do with my life.'

At that point Ishmael had to negotiate a roundabout, change lanes, read a road sign, change gear and avoid a maniac on a motorcycle. Davey took his silence for wisdom and careful consideration.

'You don't have to tell me right now. You can think about it for a while.'

Ishmael supposed he was honoured. He supposed he was flattered. He supposed this was a form of power.

'Well I do have one idea of my own,' Davey said. 'Oh, I feel silly mentioning it, but would you consider taking me on as a disciple?'

*

Major Ivan Hirst had a pretty good sort of a war. At the age of seventeen he had become second-lieutenant in the Territorials. That was in 1934. The Battle of France saw him a major. His job with the Royal Electrical and Mechanical Engineers was at first as an instrument specialist, but by 1944 he was responsible for all forms of military vehicle repair.

Now, in late 1945, the war over, but with what are becoming to seem like the real problems only just beginning, he knocks on the door of Colonel R.C. Radclyffe's office at the Zonal Headquarters of the Control Commission (British Element).

'Come in, Major Hirst. Sit down.'

Jesus, thought Ishmael, this was getting serious. He wished he had a dictionary to hand so that he could look up the full implications of what 'disciple' meant. He had never been a fan of organized religion. He was not religious. He was not organized.

'What would your being a disciple involve exactly?' he asked.

'That would be up to you. You're the boss.'

'Ah.'

'But if you'd let me make one or two suggestions . . .'

'Please go on.'

'I thought I could sit next to you, you driving, me in the passenger seat, and I'd absorb wisdom while we drove. You'd talk in that way you have and I could receive instruction. Then if you wanted some petrol putting in the car, say, or the oil checked, I'd be there to do your bidding.'

When he put it like that it sounded oddly appealing.

'Tell me about your hands,' Ishmael said. 'Are they really deadly weapons?'

'Deadly, I don't know. I did the whole course but I left without taking the exam – I wasn't happy with the standard of teaching. It seemed to neglect the spiritual dimension. So my hands aren't deadly but they could do somebody a nasty injury.'

Ishmael thought of Marilyn's mother – her swift movements, her grace, her uncanny accuracy with a claw hammer. He thought of Marilyn's father. He thought of his head making unlovely contact with a rear wing. Suddenly Davey seemed a good man to have in the team.

'All right,' Ishmael said. 'Let's give it a try. But I'd like you to remember the words of Bob Dylan: "Don't follow leaders/Watch for parking meters." '

Davey let the words wash over him.

'It doesn't rhyme,' he said.

Colonel Radclyffe sits behind a desk that displays an orderly array of maps, one telephone, in and out trays (both full), and a small potted plant.

Radclyffe, avoiding all ceremony, says to Hirst, 'Tell me about your work in Brussels, as second-in-command at the tank workshop.'

'I was works manager, in charge of all forms of repair. I had the standard British military personnel plus three hundred Belgian civilians.'

Radclyffe smiles ruefully. 'Gallant little Belgium. Hands across the sea. International co-operation. All that sort of rot, eh?'

'You could put it that way I suppose, Colonel,' Hirst replies flatly.

In July 1958 Vic Damone was riding high in the British pop charts with 'On the Street Where You Live', and the Esso Gas Research Centre published a report stating that 'Tuning into rock and roll radio stations can cost the motorist money!' The theory is that the driver is impelled to tap his foot on the accelerator in time to the incessant beat, and so waste petrol.

In that case God alone knew what kind of effect Davey's ghetto-blaster was having on Ishmael's fuel consumption. Anything that could make itself heard above the engine and wind noise from Enlightenment had to be worthy of respect, and so it was they made the trip from Cambridgeshire to Kent to the fierce accompaniment of Davey's collection of 'road music' tapes.

They had chart-bound sounds, golden oldies, blasts from the past – the works.

As they tooled down the M11 past Audley End they were born to be wild. As they covered the miles between Ugley Green and Fiddler's Hamlet they tried to get it on and they thrilled to the line that described how she was built like a car, with a hubcap diamond star halo; then miles and miles of the M25 and a lot, really an awful lot of Bruce Springsteen, endless references to shock absorbers and state troopers, girls in their best dresses and some strapping of hands across engines. The Dartford Tunnel saw Johnny Guitar Watson hitting the highway, and as they neared journey's end they asked themselves why didn't they do it in the road.

Sometimes Ishmael had a feeling they were being followed, but he shrugged it off, thinking this was no time to get paranoid.

As and when the music allowed Ishmael explained the nature of his quest to Davey. When he'd finished he said, 'Davey, I've been thinking, I really do abhor violence, you know, but I've decided that if that scumbag father of hers doesn't listen to reason he's going to have to be punished.'

'That sounds very reasonable,' Davey said.

Then he unzipped his jacket to show his tee-shirt. It had big red letters on the front that read 'LET'S DO IT TO THEM BEFORE THEY DO IT TO US'.

Ishmael realized it had been a good decision to give Davey a lift.

*

'And you made a pretty good job of it, Hirst.'

'I believe so, sir, yes.'

'Pretty bloody useful experience for when you get back to civvy street, I'd say.'

'I'm not thinking that far ahead at the moment, sir.'

'Nor me, Hirst. Tell me, have you heard of K-d-f Stadt?'

'No sir.'

'Have you heard of the K-d-f wagen?'

'The Beetle? Yes, well to the extent that I read an article in *Autocar*, but I don't know more than that. Is K-d-f Stadt where they're made?'

'Indeed, although the town is now called Wolfsburg. Forgive me if I get a little technical; the US 102nd Infantry took Fallersleben on April 10th, they were just a few miles away from the K-d-f factory but it wasn't on any of their maps so they had no idea that it was there. In fact, I'm sure they'd have ignored it completely if it hadn't been for the unpleasantness.'

Marilyn's parents, and for that matter Marilyn herself, at least for the moment, although it was Ishmael's plan to change all that, lived at 'Sorrento', Hawk's Lane, Crockenfield.

Crockenfield is built in a valley. There is a meandering river, a very rustic old bridge, an Elizabethan pub with a very big car-park. There is a number of old flint cottages whose doors open right on to the road, and a lot of new houses with double garages set back in long gardens. It's a nice place. It's well worth a visit.

Hawk's Lane runs parallel to the river but is set half-way up the valley. Detached houses are set at intervals along the lane. They have a lot of privacy. They have commanding views.

'Unpleasantness, sir?'

'The only way the Nazis could keep the factory running, producing military versions of the K-d-f wagen, Kubelwagens I think they called them, was by using forced labour, prisoners of war. When the SS guards woke up to the fact that they were smack in the middle of the advancing American and Russian forces, they very wisely did a bunk, deserted. The prisoners broke free, smashed everything they could smash, looted the town, ambushed trains and threatened to set fire to the whole town.'

'Good God.'

'Sorrento' was one of the bigger, one of the more detached houses. It was very clean, very white. It had grounds, a croquet lawn, a patio with built-in barbecue, and a small swimming pool.

The gates that met the road were open. They were white and made from two wagon wheels. The drive was steep and uphill. Ishmael drove in as quietly as he could, then turned the car around so it was pointing out of the gates if he needed to make a quick getaway. Davey turned off the music. Ishmael turned off the engine. There was no sign of a Rolls-Royce but there was a brand new Japanese jeep parked by the front door.

Ishmael and Davey remained in the car waiting for something to happen. Nothing happened.

'Turn the stereo on again,' Ishmael said.

Ted Nugent's 'Motor City Madhouse' filled the air. Something had to happen.

A woman came from round the side of the house. She might have been a housekeeper or cook. Certainly she had 'servant' written all over her.

'Turn that racket down,' she said.

It was turned down.

'What are you selling?' she asked.

Ishmael laughed a short, ironical laugh.

'I'm not selling,' he said.

71

'What happened to your car?' the woman asked, sounding genuinely concerned.

'I'm here for Marilyn,' Ishmael said, getting serious.

Clouds of gloom rolled over the woman's face.

'Oh dear. You're not going to cause trouble are you?'

'No,' said Ishmael. 'But I'm ready for it.'

'Oh dear.'

'I think I'd better talk to Marilyn's father.'

'He's at work, isn't he?'

Ishmael hadn't thought about that.

'It's four o'clock in the afternoon,' she went on. 'Why aren't you two at work?'

'There's three and a half million unemployed,' Davey snarled. 'Or hadn't you heard?'

'Would you like to see Marilyn's mother?'

Ishmael hesitated. He didn't have much faith in his ability to reach out and touch Marilyn's mother. He hadn't seen in her that capacity for communication that he'd seen in her husband.

'Can't I just see Marilyn?'

'All of which,' Radclyffe continues, 'I suspect would not have bothered the Yanks one whit if they hadn't discovered that there were thirty children of American-German engineers being held in the camps there, and God alone knew what the looters were going to do next. The 102nd Infantry moved in, shot the odd looter to show they meant business, these Yanks look after their own. The children were discovered to be all in one piece, and the next morning there were two hundred US troops with Sherman tanks occupying the place.'

'Don't be silly,' said the woman. 'Marilyn's under lock and key, had her allowance stopped.'

Ishmael's worst fears were confirmed.

'And can you be surprised? Running around the

72

country dressed like a harlot. Research she calls it. I'd give her research if she was a daughter of mine.'

'Is that Marilyn's room at the end there?'

'No, it's that one there.'

The woman pointed briefly to a dormer window set high amid eaves and chimneys. It looked impregnable.

'Here, I shouldn't have told you that. I suppose you think you're smart. What's your game, anyway?'

'I'm here for Marilyn.'

'Let's not go through it all again, love. You can't see Marilyn because she's confined to her room and you can't see her Dad because he's not here. I can ask the lady of the house if she'll see you, but I don't know that she will, and if she isn't willing to see you I'll have to ask you to park your Volkswagen elsewhere.'

'Hey,' said Davey. 'We're on a mercy errand. We park where we want to park.'

'Do you? I'll give you mercy errand.'

'Please, please,' Ishmael said, 'let's stay rational. All right, yes, I would be prepared to talk to Marilyn's mother if she has the time, if it's at all convenient, please.'

'Now that's a much nicer way of talking to people.'

'Thank you,' said Ishmael.

It was a mistake.

'And all I can say is, thank God the Americans got there before the Russians did. As things are Wolfsburg lies four kilometres from the border with the Russian Zone, and such are the vagaries of war, Hirst, that despite the fact that the Americans captured the place they've handed it over to us and now it's in the British Zone.'

'Sounds like a good thing, sir.'

'Not exactly.'

'Sir?'

Marilyn's mother received Ishmael in the library. It

seemed ironic, yet appropriate. She insisted on talking to him alone. Davey had to wait in the kitchen.

She was wearing a blue velour tracksuit, high heels and a lot of gold jewellery. Her hair and face firmly in place. It wasn't the natural look, but Ishmael supposed it was all right. She was a good-looking woman in her way. Like mother, like daughter, Ishmael mused.

She was standing in the library with a copy of *The Boys from Brazil* in one hand and a large glass in the other. Ishmael couldn't tell what was in the glass but from the way she treated it it was precious, it was alcoholic, and there was plenty of it. She didn't offer Ishmael any of it.

'Is Ishmael your real name?'

'It's real enough.'

'Marilyn's told us so much about you. We did rather seem to get off on the wrong foot last time.'

Ishmael relived the hammer hitting him in the groin.

'Rather.'

'We do worry about Marilyn.'

'You think I don't?'

'I suspect you do, but hardly in the same way, I feel.'

'I think my feelings are likely to be superior to any of yours, madam.'

Marilyn's mother dropped her glass. It smashed. Ice cubes, drink, a slice of lemon and splinters of glass bounced around on the polished wood floor.

'Would you be an angel and pick that up for me, Ishmael?'

He didn't see how he could refuse. He knelt and started gathering the debris.

'You are kind,' she said.

Then she clubbed him over the head with a soda syphon.

Radclyffe says, 'We've just bombed the factory into absolute buggery. But, frankly, it's the only decent bit of vehicle plant that we British have got. Oh yes, the bloody Americans carved it up very nicely for themselves. The American Zone just happens to contain the Mercedes, the Opel and the BMW factories, while the Russian Zone also has a BMW factory and an Auto Union plant at Zwickau.

'We're left with a more than half-bombed factory, and a pretty half-baked prototype.'

'I don't think, with respect, that you're being quite fair, sir. The prototype seems viable enough. They certainly seemed to be quite acceptable as war vehicles. Damned sturdy little beasts they are too, I'd say.'

Colonel Radclyffe allows himself a smile of gentle satisfaction.

'I see,' he says. 'So you know a good deal more about these vehicles than you were prepared to admit.'

Things moved rather rapidly for Ishmael, though he was in no state to be aware of the fact. He wasn't even conscious for some of it.

He felt the blow on the back of the head and more or less passed out, though he did have certain memories of various kinds of pain being inflicted on him while he was on the floor of the library so the unconsciousness could not have been absolute. Then he was outside the house and Marilyn's mother was attacking Enlightenment with a fierce and drunken passion. She had a sledge-hammer which she used to telling effect on every panel of the car. Pieces of chrome and glass showered from it. She had some trouble smashing the windscreen, but not too much trouble.

Ishmael saw this wrecking through a haze of concussion, and then he was bundled behind the wheel. There was much screaming along the lines of 'Never darken my doorstep again' and as a parting shot Marilyn's mother called Ishmael a sexual inadequate which he thought was unnecessary and unfair.

She returned to the house and slammed the door behind her. She probably needed a drink.

'Only an interested layman's knowledge, sir,' says Hirst. 'Honestly.'

'So, Hirst, what we have is a prototype which you are obviously rather enthusiastic about and obviously think is viable, a factory as described, and a gang of crazed POWs. Though, of course, they're "Displaced Persons" now. And this is precisely where you come in.'

The servant woman who had been watching the show came over to the car to speak to Ishmael. He had no need to wind down a window, Marilyn's mother had smashed that too.

'You really ought to be getting along now, don't you think?' said the woman.

Ishmael agreed.

And then he heard the tyres of a Rolls-Royce turning into the drive. It was Marilyn's father. Ishmael was filled with remorse. If only he had waited. If only he hadn't rushed into a quick and futile confrontation with Marilyn's mother.

Still he was not defeated. He threw open the door of Enlightenment and crossed unsteadily to the Rolls. Marilyn's father stepped out of his car.

'You again,' he said.

'Me,' said Ishmael.

Ishmael put out his hand. Marilyn's father more or less shook it. Ishmael knew he had to speak, to speak eloquently and boldly, to strike a man's heart and to change that man's mind.

'Sir,' he began. 'May I call you sir? I want from you something that is the richest prize a man can have, and yet a prize that no man can own. I speak of Marilyn. And please don't think I want to take her away from you, at least not emotionally. She will be with you always, in your heart and mind, and you in hers, if you let her be free to find her secret self . . .'

Marilyn's father wasn't especially attentive through most of the speech. He went to the boot of his car and started to take something out of it. Ishmael felt his audience slipping away from him.

'Sir, I want your daughter. Give me her hand. Give me her all.'

Marilyn's father had lost interest. Ishmael had lost more than that.

It was a shotgun that Marilyn's father had been getting from the boot of the Rolls-Royce. He loaded it. He looked about to use it. Ishmael had never faced a man with a gun before, but if he couldn't have Marilyn, what did it matter?

'Do your worst!' he cried.

'Where precisely do I come in, sir?'

'The British army will be working alongside a group of international flotsam and jetsam, some of them on the brink of madness and starvation. Your Belgian stint should stand you in good stead. Admittedly there's not much fuel or food or raw materials, and nobody's going to think very much the worse of you if you decide after a few months that the whole thing was a rotten idea in the first place. But, at the least, your job is to get some vehicles repaired so that our men can use them, get these DPs working, and while you're at it see if you can't knock together a few of these people's cars. We're crying out for any sort of motorized transport, and I was thinking that one of these Beetle things might make a rather agreeable staff car.

'See any problem at all, Hirst?'

'No, sir,' says Hirst wearily.

'I've arranged some transport for you, Hirst.'

*

Marilyn's father paced over to Enlightenment, opened the engine cover and emptied the contents of his shotgun into the air-cooled flat-four unit.

'You're the clever little sod who made off with my wallet,' he said, as though this explained something, then he too went into the house.

'You really will have to be going now,' the servant lady said.

Ishmael returned to his driver's seat and took off the handbrake. The car rolled down the slope of the drive, through the gates and on to the road. It drifted gently and unpowered for a hundred yards or more along Hawk's Lane. As the road sloped downhill it started to gain speed. He tried to brake. There were no brakes. He wrestled with the steering, tried to pull on the handbrake, and put the car in a ditch. It seemed as good a place as any.

Six

Ishmael slumped over the wheel. His arm rested on the horn boss. The horn didn't work either.

His head ached. He started to cry, but that didn't help much. Where had his eloquence been when he needed it? Come to that, where had his bloody 'disciple' been? There was no sign of Davey. He must have run away. Oh ye of little faith, but Ishmael couldn't altogether blame him.

A phone rings in the office of *Cult Car*. Terry answers it and has a conversation that Renata can't quite hear, except to notice that Terry is saying 'fuck' at regular intervals. After he's finished the call he crosses to Renata's desk, looking authentically gloomy.

'Got a scoop, chief?' Renata asks.

'The clown with the Vauxhall Velox has just wrapped it round a milk float on the way to the photo session. You're just going to have to write me another article.'

'My big break. Hope I don't blow it! What on?'

'How do I know? Three thousand words that doesn't need much in the way of picture research.'

'The big time.'

Ishmael sat for a long time, worrying how he would explain the state of the car if he phoned for the AA. He didn't know what was important any more.

A pale blue Beetle was approaching at great speed. As it got closer Ishmael could hear the savage tone of the modified engine, and at last he could see that Fat Les was driving.

The car did not appear to be slowing down, instead it appeared at one moment to be driving past at a dangerously high speed, the next moment it had stopped.

Les got out. He left the engine running. He looked at Ishmael and placed a fatherly hand through the broken window and on to his shoulder.

'Are the bastards getting you down, then?' he asked.

Terry pours himself coffee. He then does a fair impersonation of a man thinking.

'I've got it,' he says. 'Fifty Facts You Always Wanted to Know About the Volkswagen Beetle.'

'You jest,' Renata replies.

'It's got "winner" written all over it.'

'You're only saying that because you don't have to write it.'

Fat Les drove. Ishmael didn't know where. He supposed they were heading back to the railway arch, back to the kingdom. To the Zen pedestrian, as Ishmael supposed he now was, it was irrelevant. All places were one, and all of them rotten.

'I was tailing you most of the way,' Fat Les said. 'I thought you might need some help. Think I was right. I lost you after the Dartford Tunnel, then I took a wrong turning. Finished up in Sevenoaks. Nice place. Well worth a visit.'

Ishmael didn't say anything.

'We'll go back for the car tomorrow, eh? I'll get a trailer. I can't see anyone's going to nick it. I didn't think that car of yours could look any worse than it already did. I was wrong. Don't worry, son, we'll have it back on the road in no time. Better than new.'

His kindness only made Ishmael feel worse.

'Remember the old thing with the hammer.'

'Hammer?' Ishmael asked.

'You can have the same hammer all your life. You may have to replace the head a few times, you may have to replace the shaft a few times, but it's still the same hammer.

'It's the same with cars. You take old Enlightenment back there. There's nothing we can't alter, nothing we can't replace. We can strip it down to bare metal, take it apart and start again, but there's something you don't change.

'Shit, I'm not even sure that *people* have souls, so I'm not one to judge, but there's something about some motors, something in them – something I'd call soul. And when I saw that customized old rust bucket of yours, I saw it had a soul.'

'That's the nicest thing anybody's said to me in a long time,' said Ishmael.

Renata looks at the draft of the editorial which is even now withering in her 'pending' tray.

'OK, Terry, you get your Volkswagen article on two conditions. One, I don't have to write this crappy editorial. Two, if this Lamborghini turns up, and I know there are no guarantees, but if it does, then I'm the one who gets to drive it.'

Terry pulls a face, turns away, slouches over to the other side of the office and stares out of the window, a picture of Great Russian misery. In the *Cult Car* office this passes for giving in gracefully.

Driving with Fat Les was a real Zen experience. The Zen archer hits the target without aiming, but also without not aiming. He's become one with the target, therefore, to miss the thing with which you are unified is not only a contradiction in terms, it is also impossible.

So, when Fat Les was driving he didn't aim, in fact he hardly looked at the road at all. He didn't seem to look in his mirror. He didn't seem to pay much heed to traffic lights, or speed limits, or road markings saying 'Slow'. He didn't slow for corners, or junctions, or pedestrians. He juggled with a cigarette, a can of beer, a bag of salt and vinegar crisps, while at the same time trying to tune in the radio to something Wagnerian, and without letting up on the accelerator.

In an attempt to cheer up Ishmael he conducted an intense conversation about the difference in horsepower-gains various performance exhaust set-ups are likely to give, but he would break off from this at intervals and shout intense abuse at any driver who was progressing more sanely than himself.

In truth, the only time he notices other traffic is when it is in his way. His favourite advanced driving technique, when he finds a stretch of fast road, is to tuck in behind a sporty hatchback, preferably one with a few flashy accessories. He drives about eighteen inches behind the rear bumper and starts flashing his headlights madly. The other driver, feeling his virility threatened, accelerates gently thinking this is all that will be necessary, but it is not. Fat Les stays on his tail and their speeds climb, seventy-five, eighty, eighty-five. By now the driver in front realizes he is dealing with a situation not covered by the Highway Code, and he hates it. But he's still the car in front, still thinks he will be able to burn off this Volkswagen in the end. Fat Les lets him savour this feeling by dropping back a couple of feet, then a couple of yards. The guy in front starts to think the contest is over and that he's the winner. He relaxes just slightly, just too much. The Beetle pulls out to overtake, the engine takes on a new note. Suddenly, as though kicked in the backside by an invisible force, the Beetle shoots forward, passes the hatchback as if it is standing still. The look on Fat Les's face is one of complete serenity. There is no strain, no effort, just the satisfied look of one who has established his rightful place on the road, ahead of everyone else.

Renata's typewriter rattles with a quiet desperation.

FIFTY FACTS YOU ALWAYS WANTED TO KNOW ABOUT THE
VOLKSWAGEN BEETLE
ONE: The only part of a Beetle never to have been
modified in all its years of production is the rubber
seal around the engine lid.

'Now that *is* a thing I've always really wanted to
know,' Renata says to the air.

Half an hour later she is still in need of another forty-
seven facts, and even more in need of a drink. It is then
that Terry enters the office and calls her a witch. The
Lamborghini Countach has just been delivered. Renata
rushes out to it.

She straps herself in, spends a lot of time working out
what is responsible for what on the dashboard, and takes
to the road.

FACT: A recent American survey says that 11.5 per cent
of Californian teenagers lose their virginity in a
Volkswagen – over half succeeding in doing it in a
cabriolet version.
FACT: The eccentric painter and stage-designer Philip
Kaufmann became a recluse in 1972. Until his
untimely death from carbon monoxide poisoning
last year he had painted nothing but watercolours of
his 1952 split-window Beetle.

All right, so she has made up these last two facts, but
the imagination runs riot behind the wheel of a Lamborghini. And so what? Terry won't read the article, the
people who buy the magazine almost certainly won't read
it. What has she got to lose? Her journalist's integrity?
Her job?

*

'How did you learn to drive like that?' Ishmael asked Fat Les.

'Like what? I just drive normally.'

That's what Ishmael liked about Les. He was instinctive. He was a primitive.

'And I'll tell you something else,' Fat Les continued. 'In thirty years of driving I've never had an accident. Mind you, I've seen plenty.'

Renata finds the Lamborghini an animal to drive. It is sexy and black and desirable, but an animal. Renata doesn't mind. She likes animals.

Fat Les drove home via a scenic route. They stopped at a Little Chef for a homely, family-style meal. They chose the all-day breakfast.

Ishmael toyed with his mushrooms.

'What do I do about Marilyn?' he asked, not really of anyone in particular.

'Buggered if I know,' said Les. 'You must really fancy this bird.'

'I worship her,' Ishmael said. 'I've put her on a pedestal.'

'Swipe me,' said Les.

Renata has always entertained some unsound fantasies about hitch-hikers. She knows that she is more likely to find a hitch-hiker who will rob and rape her than one who is the man of her dreams, but that's how it is with fantasies. She picks up a youth. He is about seventeen, failing to grow a moustache, wearing a studded leather jacket and carrying a ghetto-blaster. He is not the man of her dreams but he doesn't look like a robber or rapist either. She tells him she is a journalist.

'That's interesting.'

Silence.

'How do you like the car?' she tries again.

'Not bad,' Davey says. 'Beetles are my favourite, though.'

The cockpit is cramped, not that the boy has much luggage, not any that Renata can see, just the ghetto-blaster and a carrier bag with some tapes in it. She hopes he at least has a pair of clean knickers.

'Now there's a coincidence,' says Renata. 'I don't suppose you have forty or so facts that I've always wanted to know about the Volkswagen Beetle.'

'Not really,' he replies, taking her very seriously. 'A friend turned me on to them, well I say friend, he's more of a mentor really. I'm on my way to find him at the moment. If you're a journalist you could write something about him. He's an amazing character.'

Davey retells Ishmael's story, from Branch Library to Nirvana, from librarian to chivalric pilgrim, the nature of the quest, the nature of the dragon, scenes of casual violence in town and country, the rescue of the fair Marilyn which must not fail.

'Are you serious?' Renata asks.

'You want to interview him or not?'

'Not. But I'd certainly be interested in doing something when you both get put behind bars.'

'What are you trying to say?'

'This friend of yours is obviously a fruitcake. What's he trying to do – become the English Don Quixote, or the next Charles Manson?'

'I think you'd better stop before you say something you regret.'

'I'm not going to regret anything. And you're even more stupid than you look if you fall for all that quasi-mystical bullshit. OK, you're young and gullible, but take it from me, kid, if there's one thing the sixties taught us it's that the kind of thing your friend's playing with just leads to a lot of bad business and a few blown minds.'

'But this isn't the sixties, you silly cow. Stop the car! You have to put up with a lot when you're hitch-hiking but I'm not going to sit here and have my most precious beliefs spat on. Let me out at that Little Chef over there.'

Ishmael looked absently through the large window. A car that was a streak of black, lacquered metal pulled up.

'What's that?' he said to Fat Les.

'Lamborghini Countach.'

The passenger door flapped open. Davey got out. He said something to the driver, the door closed, the car left. He walked into the Little Chef, sat down at Ishmael's table, expressed no surprise at his being there and said, 'Those Lambos, they're some car, pity that the people who drive them are such scumbags.'

He looked at the menu. Ishmael introduced Les and Davey to each other. At first Ishmael wasn't going to take him to task for his desertion, but as Davey sat there at the plastic table, all youthful, cocky arrogance, it all boiled up inside.

'Where were you when I needed you?' Ishmael spluttered.

'I was in the kitchen.'

'I know *that*. Why weren't you where I was?'

'I didn't see any point in us both getting smacked about.'

Ishmael fumed.

'While you were in the library getting coshed I was having a good look through the kitchen drawers. Here, I've got something for you.'

He dropped a set of keys into Ishmael's palm.

Davey said, 'A lot of people keep a spare set of house keys somewhere in the kitchen. Silly of them.'

At first Ishmael was all for returning to 'Sorrento' the moment it was dark, breaking in, and freeing Marilyn.

But Fat Les advised caution. He advised going home, having eight or nine pints of bitter and getting plastered. Ishmael tried to argue, but Fat Les was the driver, and Ishmael was persuaded that he might feel more in the mood for burglary when his pains and bruises had receded slightly.

Davey occupied the rear seat as they returned to Fat Les's arch. Davey was subdued because Fat Les wouldn't let him play any of his tapes.

'You can hear some real music when we get home,' he said, meaning Wagner.

They arrived home. Les put *The Flying Dutchman* on his stereo, opened a few four-pint cans of beer and became a very happy man.

For a time they were all happy men, then Davey became ill. Ishmael was happier longer than Davey but then the beer just seemed to make his aches and tiredness worse. He slept on a pile of secondhand tyres. It wasn't the worst place he'd ever slept.

By the time Ivan Hirst gets to Wolfsburg he is nearly forty, but he is one of those men who has always looked nearly forty. His hair is brushed and oiled into an effect of polished blackness. He has a thick, slightly wayward moustache that perches above a mouth that for preference grips a short, straight pipe.

'I say, Atkinson,' Hirst says brightly. 'Do you know why the Beetle has two tailpipes?'

Atkinson, a young lieutenant, a joiner in real life, offers, 'Something to do with the fact that it's air-cooled?'

Hirst smiles his boyish smile and says, 'No, no, they're fittings for broom handles.'

'Sir?'

'So that when the wretched things conk out you can stick a couple of broom handles up the tailpipes and use the blighter as a wheelbarrow.'

Hirst laughs with great satisfaction. This is one of his favourite jokes, used frequently and to great effect.

'But surely, sir, they're too close together.'

'It is a joke, Atkinson.'

'And surely, sir, with respect, that would only apply to a model with a soft top.'

'Carry on, Atkinson.'

When Ishmael woke up next morning he could see Fat Les fiddling with a brake drum from a Beetle. He could see Davey going through some martial-arts exercises. Ishmael was sorry he didn't have some similar form of morning discipline. He wished that Marilyn was with him. He was glad that he didn't have to go to work. He wished Enlightenment was still in one piece, but he was glad that at least he had the keys to 'Sorrento'. It was a morning of mixed blessings.

Les had made some tea. It was vile. There was nothing to eat. They began to devise a plan.

1. Les would borrow a trailer from his mate down the road.

2. They would reclaim Enlightenment, put it on the trailer, leave car and trailer with a mate of Fat Les's in Dartford.

3. They would wait until night.

4. Davey would black his face with boot polish. (Ishmael thought this was a bit excessive, but Davey insisted.)

5. They would return to 'Sorrento', Les would park a little way away, Davey and Ishmael would attempt to enter the house, preferably by the kitchen door, for which they had a key. Davey would then stand guard downstairs while Ishmael went to Marilyn's room, unlocking the door with another key from the bunch. Ishmael would enter her room, there would be a short, tearful reunion, but that would have to wait until later. They would steal

out, locking doors behind them so that Marilyn's absence would not be noticed until the next day. They would return to Dartford, pick up trailer and Enlightenment and drive on to Fat Les's railway arch.

6. Fat Les would patch up Enlightenment.

7. Ishmael and Marilyn would start a new life together.

Steps 1 to 4 presented no problem.

Colonel Radclyffe has not exaggerated the deprivations and difficulties that prevail at Wolfsburg. There are all kinds of shortage, various kinds of madness. And there is also the problem of ideological purity. The whole factory workforce is having to undergo the unlovely process of 'denazification'. Hirst has already lost a couple of his best mechanics because they retained threads of loyalty to Hitler. Among the enforced labour there are still attempts at looting, lots of petty violence and fighting, and Hirst can only partly blame them. Repatriation is starting, at least for some, for others (and there are plenty like this) there is no country that wants them. And above all, the military government can't make up its bloody mind as to whether it might not be a lot easier for all concerned simply to dismantle the whole factory and share out its assets as reparations.

Step 5 swung into action. Fat Les parked his Beetle a couple of hundred yards from the gates of 'Sorrento'. It was well hidden by hedge and an overhanging tree.

'Couldn't you park a bit nearer?' Ishmael asked.

'Why?'

'Two hundred yards is quite a long way to run if you're being chased by some irate father with a shotgun.'

'You'll be all right,' Fat Les said, reassuringly. 'That's just the sort of incentive you need. You'll be back here like a greyhound if it comes to that. But it won't, will it?'

'No, no, I hope . . . no, of course it won't.'

Sometimes there was no arguing with Fat Les.

It was midnight. Ishmael hoped that Marilyn's mother and father were heavy sleepers. He and Davey got out of the car and approached 'Sorrento'. Davey was acting nonchalant. Ishmael was trying to. He wasn't sure he had the temperament for this kind of work. His hands were visibly shaking. The gates to the house were locked. They climbed over. Davey was cat-like. Ishmael was not.

The house was in darkness. Ishmael had hoped that Marilyn's light might still be on. It wasn't.

They each had a small hand-torch. They hadn't wanted anything too bright, for fear of giving themselves away. The torches cast small pools of dirty, yellow light as Ishmael and Davey negotiated the drive. One of the pools was noticeably trembling. They rounded the house and found the kitchen door.

'Know anything about burglar alarms?' Davey asked.

Ishmael shook his head.

'Me neither,' Davey said.

Ishmael held the torch while Davey tried each of the keys in turn. None fitted. Davey held the torch while Ishmael tried. For a moment Ishmael felt blissful relief. If none of the keys fitted perhaps they could go home and try another time. Then he mentally flayed himself for his lack of purpose.

'Know what the trouble is?' Davey whispered.

Ishmael shook his head again.

'The door's not locked.'

Davey turned the handle of the kitchen door. The door opened. They went in. Davey looked around and selected a seat at the breakfast bar.

'OK, Batman,' he said. 'Go get her.'

Ishmael couldn't help thinking that Davey sometimes had a very flippant attitude for a disciple.

In 1943 the Humber Company, by arrangement with the

Ministry of Supply, published a detailed technical report and assessment on a modified Volkswagen captured in the Libyan desert in the aftermath of Alamein – a German Light Aid Detachment Vehicle Type VW82. The report, which took eight months to compile, eschews wartime austerity in its production. It contains sixty-four glossy, foolscap pages, clothbound like some particularly rare collectors' edition. With patriotic obsessiveness the report details the complete dismantling of the vehicle, the weight of every component is noted, every type of metal is analysed. One is fascinated to learn that the vehicle's actual unladen weight is 14cwt 3qr, even though the vehicle's identification plate states that the figure is 13cwt, 1qr, 26lb.

A strange house at night, in darkness. Things change their shape, their nature. A grandfather clock becomes a hooded figure, a telephone table becomes a small vicious animal, a portrait on the wall becomes the face of God or the devil.

The hallway and stairs held few horrors. They were thickly carpeted. It was easy to walk quietly. He climbed the stairs which ended in a long landing that disappeared round corners at each end. Ishmael knew that Marilyn's room must be one floor higher than this, so around one of these corners there had to be another set of stairs leading up to Marilyn.

On the landing he could see perhaps four doors and noticed, with a sudden acute sick feeling, that light was visible round one of them.

He flattened himself against one of the walls, just the way they do in films. Then he could hear a voice behind the door. It was a woman's voice and it was singing 'Send in the Clowns'. It sounded like Marilyn's mother. The singing became louder and it was obvious that she was very drunk. She didn't have a bad voice.

Then a light appeared under one of the other doors. There were the sounds of someone getting out of bed, of moving to the door and opening it. Ishmael hid round a corner of the landing – no staircase there. The second bedroom door opened and heavy, angry footsteps marched to the first bedroom. It was Marilyn's father. Separate bedrooms, eh? He flung open his wife's door. They had a loud, colourful exchange in which he said she was a disgrace to motherhood and womanhood, and if she wanted to sing she should go down the pub which was where she belonged in any case. She said anybody would take to drink if they had to live with him, and then she taunted him about the size of his penis. Ishmael felt she got the better of this exchange. Marilyn's father stormed back to his own bedroom. His door slammed. His light snapped off.

The door to Marilyn's mother's bedroom remained open. She slouched in the doorway in a drunken but appealing fashion. Ishmael thought he had stayed out of sight while the previous scene had been played, but now it seemed he had been wrong. She had seen him. She started speaking to him. At first he thought she must be talking to herself, but it soon became obvious she was actually speaking to him.

'That was a close thing,' she said. 'You found the door I left open for you, Gerry. I'm glad you got my message. I'm glad you came. I did get your name right? It is Gerry? From the television repair shop. Don't just stand there, silly, come in, have a drink.'

Ishmael went in.

What especially interests Major Ivan Hirst about the Humber report are the 'purely personal views' of the chaps in the Engineering Division. 'Looking at the general picture we do not consider that the design represents any special brilliance . . . and it is suggested that it is not to be regarded as an example of first-class modern design to be copied by British Industry.'

'Well,' thinks Hirst, 'there was a war on, after all. I suppose it must have been good for morale to know that the enemy was driving around in vehicles "without any special brilliance".'

The bedroom was a soft-pornographer's dream of heaven. The concept resembled a hall of mirrors decked out with purple, black and chrome accessories. The bed was vast and a tangle of silk and fur, and Marilyn's mother, in order that she might contrast nicely with the rest of the room, was wearing a couple of flaps of white silk.

But Ishmael didn't get much of a chance to look around the room, and Marilyn's mother didn't get much of a chance to look round him, because she reached for the dimmer-switch and the room descended into romantic dusk.

She relaxed on the bed. Ishmael tried to keep his face averted.

'Make us a couple of drinks,' she said.

He went to the Chinese sideboard, black and glossy, and took as much time as he could pouring two whiskies. It enabled him to keep his back to the bed.

'When I saw you loading those heavy televisions into that van, I thought "I've got to have him". That's the kind of woman I am, Gerry. I take what I want, Gerry, and I want you – urgently.'

Ishmael continued taking his time with the drinks.

'God, you are the strong silent type, aren't you?'

Ishmael could hear her settling herself on the bed. He glanced over his shoulder and saw that she had tossed her head back into the sea of pillows, and that her eyes were closed in anticipation of some impending ecstasy. He filled her glass to the brim. He took it over to the bed and placed it in her hand. Some of the whisky spilled on to her chest.

With eyes still closed she knocked back half the drink then said, 'Do it to me, stud. Do it now and do it hard.'

Now it is 1946. It is 'Post-war'. Why then, Hirst asks himself, does this Humber attitude persist? He has now in his possession a volume called *Investigation into the Design and Performance of the Volkswagen or German People's Car*. It reprints the Humber report and compares that modified military vehicle with a side-valve Hillman Minx Mark III, and also with a post-war Volkswagen which has recently been sent from Wolfsburg to Humber's experimental department.

For Hirst it is like reading the school report of his first-born. At first the report seems favourable, favourable enough certainly for Sir William Rootes to arrange a visit to Wolfsburg. There are all sorts of options that Sir William might take up. He could have the rights to manufacture the Volkswagen, in Germany, in Britain, modified as he sees fit, on almost any terms he cares to name.

The visit is brief and formal, and at the end of it Sir William announces that he does not want Wolfsburg, does not want the Volkswagen, does not want any part of them, not at any price, not even as a gift, not even if you paid him.

Later the men from Ford will say much the same, and by then Hirst will have stopped being surprised. Morale is as much an issue in peace as it is in war. Of course one doesn't fight a world war merely to decide at the end of the day that actually the Germans had one or two good ideas.

Ishmael was shocked. Perhaps he shouldn't have been. Perhaps he was not quite as liberal as he liked to think. Of course he was all for Marilyn's mother being who and what she wanted to be. However, it still came as a bit of a stunner to be mistaken for a bit of rough by one's prospective mother-in-law.

He did think, briefly, about doing it now and doing it hard, if for no other reason than it would keep her quiet and that she might fall asleep afterwards, but he decided against it. He'd had a rough couple of days. He was nervous as a kitten just being in the house, never mind her bedroom, so he doubted that he would be anybody's idea of a stud. Also, he wasn't Gerry. Also, although he knew that love and hate are often like two ponies in the same harness, he didn't find it especially easy to have any sexual feelings for a woman who had already beaten him up twice. Also, he wondered whether it might technically be a form of incest.

Fortunately alcohol came to the rescue. Marilyn's mother finished her drink. He gave her his own drink and that went rapidly in the same direction.

'Come down here, damn you,' she said. 'I want to get a good look at you.'

She yanked him by the shoulders and he fell clumsily across the purple sheets. She gave him an unco-ordinated, but deeply-felt French kiss. Ishmael felt safe enough kissing. While he was involved in that activity his face would be too close for Marilyn's mother to focus on.

'Oh, that's nice,' she moaned when they broke for breath. 'That's very nice.'

Then she pulled away. She held his face in her hands and looked into his eyes.

'You're not Gerry at all,' she said. 'You're . . .'

And then she passed out.

It was time Ishmael had a piece of luck.

Hirst realizes, and is frequently reminded, that technology is no more apolitical than art or military science. And if we find it hard enough to hate the sin but love the sinner, how can we hate the sinner yet still want to develop one of his pet projects?

One way is to assert that the Volkswagen was the product of Ferdinand Porsche, rather than of Adolf Hitler. Dr Porsche has just been made sharply aware that engineering is not an abstract or neutral activity. If, before the war, he was unaware of Hitler's use of motorsport as propaganda for international Nazism, his sudden incarceration by the French as a war criminal must have removed the scales from his eyes.

The French, of course, do not seriously believe that Dr Porsche is a war criminal in any true sense, in fact they find his activities in the war so atrocious that they try to enlist his help in developing the Renault 4CV.

Ishmael left Marilyn's mother to her dreams, gently closed her bedroom door and went in search of the staircase to Marilyn's room. It was not hard to find. It was short, steep and led only to one door. He searched among his keys and found the one that opened the door. He turned it. The door opened. He stepped inside.

'Marilyn,' he said, in a loud whisper.

He could make out a pile of clothes on the floor. He could make out the bed, and asleep in the bed, her hair upon the pillow like a sleepy golden storm, Marilyn.

He shook her gently and placed a kiss on her cheek. Her eyes opened, registered terror, then recognition, then terror again, then they refused to commit themselves.

'Oh, Marilyn, it's been so long.'

'My God, what are you doing here?'

'I'm your knight in shining armour. I've come to rescue you.'

'That's very nice, but . . .'

'You don't need to say anything. Words are useless at times like this. It's all right, I know what's been happening. How could they lock you up? How patriarchal can they get?'

'I'm sure Daddy thinks he has my best interests at heart.'

'Do you?'

'Well, usually.'

Marilyn turned on her bedside lamp. Ishmael could see she was naked in bed. It had never been like this with Debby.

'How did you get in?' Marilyn demanded. 'How did you even know where I lived? How did you unlock my door? How are you ever going to get away with this?'

'There's a fast car waiting. I have friends ready to take you away from all this.'

'Where to?'

'There's a railway arch I suppose we could stay in.'

Marilyn wasn't impressed.

'Or, or, I've met some people on a commune.'

'Now I've always wanted to stay on a commune. It could really help me with my novel. You haven't asked me how my novel's going.'

Ishmael asked how her novel was going.

'It's so hard, you know. Every day I have to sit down, confront the empty page and fill it. It's so hard. It's amazing that anybody can ever do it.'

Ishmael had been a librarian. It had ceased to amaze him a long time ago.

'I was wondering whether it might make a screenplay,' Marilyn continued. 'Because it's a very visual subject – the road, space, the land, the air. I can see it in filmic terms. The casting would be very important.'

'Please, Marilyn, we really have to get going.'

'*Have* to?'

'There's so much to explain and this isn't the time or the place.'

'Before I run into the night with some man I hardly know I want a few explanations. Or do you think I'm being unreasonable?'

Ishmael gave all the explanations he could. The most important being that he worshipped her, that he put her on a pedestal, and that he wanted to spend the rest of his life with her.

'In a railway arch,' Marilyn snorted.

'Or a commune. Or anywhere so long as we're together.'

'It's just sudden, that's all. But I suppose it might be fun. At least until I go back to Oxford at the end of the vac. A real writer can't afford to turn down any experience. You're on.'

She packed a small case, put on leopardskin trousers and a dinner jacket, and they were ready to go. They would have made it too, if they hadn't run into Gerry the television repair man.

Colonel Radclyffe tells Hirst bluntly, 'The Russians have stationed two officers and thirty men in Wolfsburg, and if the worst comes to the worst they're quite capable of marching into the factory and waltzing off with whatever "reparations" take their fancy.'

'They wouldn't dare,' Hirst says.

'Major Hirst, I don't really think there's anyone in England who would relish an international incident with an ally over a few presses and the odd generator.'

'We're not talking about a few presses and the odd generator. We're talking about a modern, viable motor factory, perfectly capable of manufacturing high quality vehicles in bulk.'

Ishmael and Marilyn were creeping along the landing in one direction when they encountered someone doing precisely the same from the opposite direction. They were soon to learn that it was Gerry, Marilyn's mother's bit of rough, but at that moment they saw only a towering heavily-built stranger carrying a bottle of Southern Comfort and two tumblers.

Marilyn screamed, Ishmael let out a yell, and Gerry the

television repair man dropped his bottle and glasses.

The light was switched on in Marilyn's father's room and seconds later they were confronted by the man himself. He switched on a lot of lights and covered all three of them with a shotgun.

'In there,' he said.

Ishmael was back in the library.

'You might as well take a seat,' Marilyn's father said. 'You're not going anywhere, at least not yet.'

The three captives sat in a row on a red velour settee.

'I can explain,' Marilyn said.

'*I* can explain,' her father bawled. 'I have one man trying to steal my daughter. I have another attempting to have sleazy sex with my wife. The two of you break into my house . . .'

'Steady on,' Gerry said. 'Nobody *broke* in. Your missus left the back door open. I can see why you're a bit upset.'

'A BIT UPSET! Do you know how it feels to have your territory invaded? Your own house? Your castle? Do you know how it feels to discover that your wife has become a nymphomaniac lush? To have a daughter who'd rather stay in a seedy motel with some lunatic in a Volkswagen than stay with her own father? Can you imagine how that feels?'

'Yes, sir,' Ishmael said. 'I think I probably can imagine. I think I can really empathize with that.'

'SHUT UP! SHUT UP YOU IMBECILE!'

Ishmael shut up.

'A Volkswagen. A German car. Who won the war?'

'We did,' Ishmael said helpfully.

'Did we? I could pick up the phone, call the police, tell them I've caught a couple of thieves. It would take them hours to get here. There'd be a hundred different forms of bureaucracy, and at the end of the day the courts would pat you on the head and tell you not to do it again. More important it would come out that I was a cuckold, that my daughter hated me, that I couldn't even keep my own back door locked. How do you imagine that would feel?'

'Reckon it'd be a real sickener,' Gerry said. 'So we'll call it quits, eh?'

Colonel Radclyffe plays his trump card.

'Do you think, Hirst, that you know more about motor production than Sir William Rootes?'

'In this limited field of operation, yes.'

'By God, Hirst, I like your spirit. Prove it then. Make a success of Wolfsburg. The Russians won't have the bloody nerve to dismantle a factory operated by the British that's producing a thousand cars a month.'

'A thousand.'

'You get production to that level and nobody is going to take your pet factory away from you, Hirst. I'll see to that.'

'Quits? I don't quit. I'm going to carry on until I win. Do you know how it is once you're successful in this world? No, I don't suppose you do. Once you've got your own business, once you're a public figure, with your own Rolls-Royce, do you think people come up, slap you on the back and say, well done old chap? They do not. Instead the pygmies, the parasites, just try to destroy you. They try to ruin your business, take your wife, vandalize your Rolls-Royce. They try to drag you down to their stinking level, but I'm not going down to your level.'

'Daddy, nobody's trying to drag you down. You're a highly respected man. You're too good a man to be threatening people with your shotgun in the middle of the night.'

Ishmael liked this development. If they were going to emerge from 'Sorrento' unscathed, Marilyn was the one most likely to effect it.

'I'll thank you for a little respect,' her father snapped. 'I'll thank you to keep quiet and speak when you're spoken to like a decent daughter should.'

'Don't come the heavy father with me,' Marilyn said, adding, 'I'll say what I like and I don't need your permission, you old fart. Fuck you.'

Ishmael's hopes drooped. He started to get fatalistic. Would he be arrested? Would he be shot? Would he live or die? It was all in the hands of fate. It was all in the hands of Marilyn's father.

Marilyn's father said, 'I'm going to let you go.'

'Well done, chief,' Gerry said. 'Very good decision.'

'SHUT UP!'

Gerry shut up.

'I'll let you go, and I'm going to call a few friends of mine, a few other members of the Crockenfield Blazers.'

Crockenfield Blazers?

Marilyn said, 'They're a group of mad fascist bastards who drive Range Rovers, play at being country squires, and shoot things.'

'Tonight they'll just be shooting at two things,' her father chuckled.

'Hey, play the white man,' said Gerry. 'I didn't even get as far as the bedroom door.'

'You didn't miss much,' Marilyn's father said.

Having been beyond the bedroom door Ishmael thought Gerry had probably missed a lot, but he held his tongue.

'The Crockenfield Blazers enjoy a bit of sport, even if it is the middle of the night.'

He put down the shotgun and picked up the phone.

'Robin, I know it's late, I've caught two intruders. No, it's not a police matter. I'm about to let them out. Phone round the others will you and we'll give these two quite a send off. I don't know whether we'll kill 'em or not, as in all hunting they have more than a sporting chance. Well then, the hunt is on.'

'Daddy, this is absurd.'

'Get to your room, Marilyn, and stay there. I wouldn't want to have to shoot my own daughter.'

'You're insane, Daddy, genuinely insane.'

Since this assessment appeared to be perfectly correct she went to her room.

'I'll be there in a moment to lock you in again.'

Then he turned to Gerry the television repair man and Ishmael.

'You'd better start running,' he said.

They started running.

Hirst rapidly learns the value of food and blankets. With these he can buy the labour and expertise of key personnel. A coal train is 'diverted' to fuel the power station that serves Wolfsburg. The military government is persuaded to bring to life the factories which manufacture essential Volkswagen supplies.

On 1 April 1946 Major Ivan Hirst sends a signal to Colonel R.C. Radclyffe. It reads 'Target Achieved'.

Hirst is photographed behind the wheel of the thousandth Beetle. The production line is decked with foliage, the nearest thing they could find to bunting. Hirst has a bottle of light ale to celebrate, lights a pipe, and has to be very careful indeed not to let his men see how his eyes are watering with pride.

Gerry the television repair man was gone in an instant, knocking over small items of furniture as he went.

Ishmael left the house as calmly as he could. There was no sign of Davey but he trusted that Fat Les and his fast Beetle were still where he had left them. They would have to leave without Marilyn but at least he wouldn't be shot and they would live to fight another day.

As he climbed over the gates of 'Sorrento' he could already hear shots being fired. They weren't being fired in anger, more in fun. These Crockenfield Blazers moved fast and Crockenfield was not a big village. The shots did not come from far away. Then dogs started to bark and car horns could be heard from different parts of the valley.

Part of him was surprised to find that Fat Les was still there. The way the evening had been progressing he almost expected to find nothing more than a few tyre tracks. But the car was there and Fat Les was behind the wheel, picking at something under his shirt.

'What are those shots?' he asked. 'Where's the bird? Where's Davey? What's happening?'

'Marilyn's locked in her room. God knows where Davey is and those shots belong to a bunch of nutters who are looking to shoot me and a television repair man.'

'Explain.'

Ishmael explained rapidly.

'What a fuck up,' Fat Les said.

'Thank God we've got a fast getaway car.'

'This father of hers is starting to get right on my tits,' Fat Les said thoughtfully. 'I think it's time that rich ponce was sorted out.'

'Another time. Let's live to fight another day.'

'What's wrong with fighting today?'

'I think we'd lose,' Ishmael said.

'Not with these,' said Fat Les, and he smiled a wicked smile.

Winners and losers. After the war. The Volkswagen factory is given back to the Germans. On 1 January 1948 Heinz Nordhoff takes up the post of general manager of Volkswagenwerk. He is a former member of the Opel board, he visited America in the thirties to study marketing and mass production, and he spent the war in charge of the Opel truck factory in Brandenberg. His credentials are in order. He is as untainted by Nazism as any German industrialist is likely to be.

The factory will remain under British control until the September of the following year, but the principle is established. We fight, we win, and when the spoils of victory appear worthless we hand them back to the losers and see what they can do with them.

On the back seat of Fat Les's Beetle there was a crate containing milk bottles filled with some kind of clear liquid.

'I haven't been sitting here twiddling my thumbs,' Fat Les said. 'I thought these might come in handy.'

The smell of petrol drifted from the car.

'Petrol bombs?' said Ishmael. 'I think you know what I'm going to say about violence.'

'You make me a bit vexed sometimes, Ishmael, you really do. Some bunch of chinless wonders are trying to shoot the arse out from under you and you start getting ethical.'

Suddenly Ishmael knew Fat Les was right. He had whetted Ishmael's almost blunted purpose.

'Show some spirit, son.'

'Yes,' Ismael said.

'Show some backbone. Show some balls.'

'Yes,' said Ishmael. 'Yes indeed.'

Fat Les saw that Ishmael's face was transformed into a mask of determined anger, a touch of heroism, a touch of madness.

'That's my boy,' Fat Les said.

They drove to the gates of 'Sorrento'. Marilyn's father was just leaving the house. It had taken him some time to lock up Marilyn. He was walking down the drive, wearing a dressing-gown and wellingtons, his shotgun in his hand. Of course, the moment he saw a Beetle parked at his front gate he lost control. He fired wildly and missed completely.

'That fucker's trying to shoot my motor,' Fat Les said. 'That's strictly out of order.'

He got out of the car, hid behind a hedge, fiddled with bottles, bits of rag and a Zippo lighter, then hurled two petrol bombs over the hedge. A curve of flickering light arched through the night, hitting the drive and exploding into orange and black.

'Well done,' said Ishmael. 'Can I throw the next one?'

Nordhoff makes a number of extraordinary and, it will be proved, brilliant decisions. First he re-establishes contact with Ferdinand Porsche, appointing him as design consultant and paying his company a royalty on every Beetle produced. (The French had to release Porsche eventually.)

Nordhoff then decides, like Henry Ford of old, that Volkswagen will be a one-model manufacturer, and, more importantly for the cult status of the Beetle, and although he is prepared for some gentle refining of the body design, he wants to keep the old shape. Evolution, not revolution. He sees himself as a polisher of Dr Porsche's diamond, not as a cutter.

The rest is automobile history – constant refinement but the soul remains the same, that and phenomenal production figures:

1948	19,244
1949	46,146
1950	81,979
1954	202,174
1956	333,190

These are more than just damned lies. By 1956 Germany has replaced Britain as Europe's top motor manufacturer. The 100,000th Beetle was completed on 4 March 1950. By August 1955 the figure had reached one million. Between 1965 and 1971 the best part of 7 million Beetles had been manufactured. And in Mexico in May of 1981 there are celebrations for the production of the 20 millionth Beetle. Ivan Hirst is in attendance. He allows himself more than a light ale.

Ishmael stood at the gates of 'Sorrento', milk bottle in hand.

'We're ready for you,' he yelled. 'There's no need to hunt us down. We're here.'

'Nicely put,' said Fat Les.

'You lot make me sick,' Ishmael continued. 'You people with your Range Rovers and your credit cards. Let's see what you're made of.'

The petrol explosion had acted as a signal for the Crockenfield Blazers. Ishmael and Fat Les would very soon see what they were made of. Headlamps shone across the valley. Lower, by the bridge and the river, excited dogs ran and howled. Ishmael was ready. From the darkness they could suddenly see two pairs of rapidly approaching headlights. The cars were driving towards Ishmael and Fat Les, side by side, one car driving down the wrong side of the road. The lights were on full beam. Their horns were blaring. Somebody leaned out of one of the cars and fired a shotgun.

Ishmael arched backwards then flung a petrol bomb into the path of the two advancing cars. Flame erupted in the centre of the road and the two cars plunged into the hedges at the sides to avoid the explosion.

'Feels good, doesn't it?' Fat Les said.

Ishmael had to agree. They got in the car.

'Where are we going?' Ishmael asked.

'Not far, look ahead.'

On 17 January 1949 the Holland America Line's ship *Westerdam* arrives in New York. In its hold is a grey Beetle saloon, chassis number 1-090 195, engine number 1-120 847. It belongs to Ben Pon who has been sent to America by Nordhoff to interest dealers in becoming agents for Volkswagen in America. He can hardly stir the slightest interest.

As he circulates New York dealers, who are anticipating an explosion of affluence, of fins and chrome, a casting-off of austerity in favour of motor design that is slick, erotic and occasionally laughable, Pon must surely have thought that Sir William Rootes, and Ernest Breech of Ford who said the Beetle was 'not worth a damn', were being proved horribly right. If nothing else these men must have known their market. The response he gets is always the same. Who won the war? We beat the bastards fair and square, now we're supposed to buy their cars so that they can rebuild their economy. What do they take us for? Bums?

There was a Range Rover parked a little way ahead. Two men were standing beside it. One of them shouted, 'Stop the car. Stop right where you are.' Fat Les stopped the car. It seemed to make everyone happy.

The other man called, 'Get out. Let's have a look at you.'

They got out to be looked at.

'They don't look like very much to me,' one of the Range Rover men said.

These two didn't have shotguns. One had a fairly savage-looking piece of chain, the other was carrying a piece of wood about the size and shape of a cricket bat, but it was jagged with nails sticking out of it.

'They must be the poor relations,' Fat Les said.

The two pairs of men stood about a cricket pitch's length apart, gunslingers at a double shoot-out.

'We may not look like much,' Ishmael said, 'but you'd be surprised. You know the problem with chains and bits of wood is that you have to get close before you can use them. You're not going to get close.'

Suddenly there were petrol bombs in Fat Les and

107

Ishmael's hands. They threw them. One landed on the roof of the Range Rover, the other just in front of it. The two men ran and dived for cover. It took a while for their vehicle to catch fire, but catch fire it did.

'Had enough yet?' Fat Les asked.

'Not nearly enough,' said Ishmael.

'That's my boy.'

Then they heard the sound of a two-tone horn. Whether it was police, fire or ambulance they didn't know, but it was time to be going. Fat Les took the remaining bottles out of the car, dropped them in the middle of the road to form a zebra crossing of petrol and broken glass. He threw a piece of burning rag at the petrol. A sheet of flame danced satisfyingly from the tarmac. They returned to the Beetle, drove round the wreck of the Range Rover and set off again into some unimaginable future of love, revenge, class warfare and oral sex.

Seven

Fat Les drove in his inimitable way. At times Ishmael had the feeling again that they were being followed, but nobody in their right mind would take the kind of risks necessary to keep up with Fat Les. Marilyn's father was not, of course, in his right mind, but Ishmael would surely have spotted a Rolls-Royce on their tail.

'Where are we going?' Ishmael asked.

'I want to see the sea,' Fat Les replied.

'Right,' said Ishmael. 'Back to the old collective unconscious.'

'Yeah.'

'This has been a strange night,' Ishmael said, unnecessarily.

'It was the best,' said Fat Les. 'Best night I've had since I was a kid.'

'But it does show that violence begets violence.'

'Yeah, there's no arguing with that.'

'It turns men into beasts. It's the death of rationality. And yet, and yet . . .'

'Yeah, fun isn't it?'

'No, not fun, not fun at all; but tonight with the danger and the threat of mayhem, the smell of death and petrol in the air, well it certainly made me feel *alive*.'

'There is no life without adventure,' said Fat Les.

Ben Pon manages at last to sell his grey Beetle at only a slight loss, and returns home. A little later Nordhoff makes his own trip to America, but lacking the confidence to take an actual car he contents himself with a sheaf of photographs. He does find somebody prepared to become Volkswagen's official American importer. In 1950 there are a grand total of 157 Volkswagens registered in the United States.

Fat Les and Ishmael headed for Brighton. Fat Les had been a mod in his earlier years and had a few memorable fights with rockers and police on Brighton beach. For him this was a Proustian journey.

'We'd missed the war. We were too young for the army, so we had to make our own amusement. We had to fight among ourselves. We fought them on the beaches, in the transport caffs, in the car-parks. Happy days.'

'I can imagine,' Ishmael said, though he couldn't.

'We rode scooters, wore suits, took pills. What did you do in your youth, Ishmael?'

'I did my O-levels, went out with Debby, went to see groups at the City Hall. I never had a youth, really.'

'Poor sod. Is that what you're trying to do now? Trying to recapture a youth you never had?'

'No,' Ishmael said. 'Youth's all about having fun. I'm not just having a good time now. I'm looking for spiritual advancement.'

'Isn't fun a form of spiritual advancement?'

Ishmael had to think about that.

The Volkswagen's conquest of America will require a very slick and thorough marketing campaign. In 1959 the advertising agency of Doyle Dane Bernbach takes on the Volkswagen account in the United States.

Despite being the third name in the company title, Bill Bernbach is the genius in the side.

An English graduate from New York University, he is at heart a copywriter, but a copywriter with an unfailing instinct for integrating words and pictures.

He gets to work at nine, goes home at five. He is a brilliant maverick who loves his family.

He carries with him a card that he looks at from time to time, especially when facing some client with whom he particularly disagrees.

The card reads, 'Maybe he's right.'

They were parked on the high sea-front at Brighton. There was a wide road, a pavement, a wall, then a sudden drop down to another road at beach level. They looked out to sea. They were drinking Colt 45. If it isn't cold, it isn't Colt. It was cold. Ishmael was shattered, freezing and nauseous, and a long way from home, yet for all that he felt at one with it all.

'To be at one with it all is to be very fucked up,' said Fat Les.

'Do you feel at one with it all, Les?'

'Sure.'

It was three in the morning but the town was not quiet. There were still drunks and loving couples wandering the streets, cars still drove past.

'We couldn't have been followed, could we?' Ishmael said. 'For one thing they'd have caught us by now.'

'You worry too much,' said Fat Les.

Then a four-wheel-drive Japanese jeep flashed past. At first it meant nothing to Ishmael, then it stirred a memory. Was it the one that had been parked outside 'Sorrento'? It looked similar, the colour might have been the same, but the same could have been said for plenty of other cars. Ishmael was getting paranoid.

But then perhaps he had reason to be paranoid. The jeep had driven past at some speed, then turned a corner and gone out of sight. Fat Les and Ishmael continued drinking their beers and looking out to sea. The jeep came by again, slower this time as though the driver was looking them over, though not slow enough for Ishmael to see who was

111

driving. It drove past and turned the corner again.

'Probably a couple of Brighton wide-boys who feel like picking on drunks,' Fat Les said. 'Are you ready for trouble?'

'I could live without it,' Ishmael replied.

'Yeah, but you could live better with it.'

Bill Bernbach knows it isn't going to be easy to sell the Volkswagen in America.

Voluptuous metal, silvered trim, enough room to have an orgy on the back seat – this is what the public thinks it wants. Bill Bernbach is about to change all that. The public never know what they want until somebody tells them.

Bernbach tells them that this car is eccentric, ornery, a lemon. 'It's ugly but it gets you there.' He makes owning a Volkswagen an act of protest against the excesses of Detroit, against vulgarity, greed and conspicuous consumption.

He tells them that Volkswagen is the car of the nonconformist. And in America there are millions of non-conformists, all waiting for a product they can buy that will confirm their individuality. Millions.

The jeep came round again. It approached along the straight sea-front road, and then it stopped, perhaps fifty yards away. The headlights were turned off. Ishmael still hoped he was mistaken. He hoped it was neither wide-boys, nor Marilyn's father. Couldn't it just be a couple out for a late night look at the sea? He couldn't see the faces of the people in the jeep, but it did look like a man and a woman. Was it Marilyn's mother and father, the old team back together, united by a shared desire to hit him some more?

The driver's and passenger's doors opened simultaneously. Ishmael was ready. Fat Les was eager. A man and woman stepped from the jeep; on the passenger's side

Davey, on the driver's side Marilyn.

'Stone the bleedin' crows,' said Fat Les.

Ishmael had to agree.

'Nice diversion,' said Davey.

'What?'

'The Molotov cocktails – a really good tactic. With all that mayhem going on I could crash about inside the house, make all the noise I wanted, and Marilyn's old man wasn't going to notice. I had to break down the door to get Marilyn out of her bedroom, but apart from that it was easy.'

'We stole the jeep – though it wasn't really stealing, Marilyn knew where the keys were. The only trouble we had was keeping up with you two. But once we saw that you were heading for Brighton that was easy too. We knew we'd find you.'

'It's so good to have you here,' Ishmael said to Marilyn.

'Looks like it was meant to be,' Marilyn replied.

'Are you sure *you* weren't followed?' Fat Les asked.

'You seem to have done a reasonable job of immobilizing half the motor transport in Crockenfield,' Marilyn said.

Davey said, 'And her Dad's not going anywhere in his Roller until he's got the sugar out of his petrol tank.'

They celebrated with a few more cans of Colt 45. Taking everything into account it had been a successful quest. It hadn't gone exactly according to plan, but Ishmael had, by however indirect a method, achieved everything he had set out to.

'And what do we do now?' Davey asked.

At first he appeared to be putting the question in general, to everyone, but then Ishmael realized he was only addressing *him*.

'I don't know,' Ishmael said. 'What should we do now, Les?'

'Don't look at me,' Fat Les said. 'How should I know?

113

You tell us. After all, you're our leader.'

Bernbach decides that the Volkswagen shall be an East Coast car, a snob car, a holier than thou car. The man who owns a Volkswagen is above all this bullshit whereby you measure a man's cock by the size of his car, the size of his ego and his salary.

A year is supposed to be a long time in American automobile production, too long a time for a manufacturer to go without making a few styling changes, each year demanding a new model. Bill Bernbach is going to change that.

A full-page newspaper ad shows a man and his Volkswagen. The man is lean and young and he is not smiling. He doesn't look like a professional model. He isn't supposed to. His name is Michael Kennedy. He looks like he could be a college professor, an aeronautics engineer, even one of a new breed of hard-edged stand-up comedians. The suit is tight. The tie is thin. He's even wearing glasses.

The caption tells us that the Volkswagen he's leaning against is made up from a 1947 body, a '55 chassis, engine and doors, '56 seats, '58 bumpers, '61 tail lights, a '62 fender, a '63 front end, and a '65 transmission.

Yes, the Volkswagen is the same, year in year out. Something constant in a world of planned obsolescence.

The campaign tells us that high volume can be consistent with high quality, that cultural enhancement need not be elitist; though Hitler, of course, got there first with both these thoughts.

The Volkswagen is the hero of the advertising campaign.

A leader? Ishmael? He who had never done more than supervise one part-time member of staff at the library. He didn't want to be in charge of anyone's life but his own.

114

He didn't mind being able to exert a little influence now and again, but he wasn't sure he wanted to lead anyone. So he said that everybody should get some sleep. This seemed a nicely modest first piece of leadership. Fat Les and Davey slept in the Beetle. Ishmael tried to sleep with Marilyn in the jeep. Sleep would not come. The front seats were too hard and the benches in the back were too narrow. So they had to talk to each other.

'Alone at last,' said Ishmael.

'I wish we were in some cheap motel,' Marilyn said. 'I wish we had some shoplifted smoked salmon and champagne, and that I was showing you my tattoo.'

It sounded all right to Ishmael.

'How do you want to die, Ishmael?' she asked.

'I don't know. I'm still trying to work out how to live. I don't think about it.'

'I think about it,' she said. 'I see my body thrown through the windscreen of a speeding car. They pull me from the wreckage, the jugular vein is severed but the face remains serene, the make-up is still perfect.

'I see myself slumped over a table in a waterfront bar. The body is ageing but it's still appealing enough in tight black lace and fishnet. The face is wrinkled, but the eyes are as sensual and as beckoning as ever. There is an empty brandy bottle on the table. The regulars see me unconscious, "That's Marilyn for you," they say with affection. "Dead drunk again." But then one of them touches my skin, as pale and cold as porcelain, and finds that I am just dead.

'I see a hotel room, very modern, very dark. The curtains are drawn, the television is showing *Pandora's Box*. The bed is tangled in an aftermath of passion. My beautiful corpse lies at an angle across the bed, in a posture that is at once impossible and yet impossibly provocative. My hair cascades over my face. One red high heel is still on, my red silk camisole seems perfect but for the one small bullet hole.

'That's the way I see it.'

'I just want to die wise,' said Ishmael, but he was more than half asleep.

A television commercial. The funeral motorcade of Maxwell E. Staveley, whose will is being read out in voice-over. He leaves his wife a calender, his sons fifty dollars each in dimes, his business partner nothing. But nephew Harold who has oft times said, 'Gee, Uncle Max, it sure pays to own a Volkswagen,' gets the entire fortune of one hundred billion dollars.

Virtue rewarded – the American way.

Next morning the four of them had breakfast together in a sea-front cafe. Ishmael found it a difficult meal to begin with. The others were still keen for Ishmael to do some leadership. But once he put his mind to it it wasn't so very hard. He decided that Fat Les should teach Davey everything he knew about Volkswagens. He realized this might take years but they could start by rebuilding Enlightenment.

He decided Marilyn would not be at home in a railway arch, but also that the time was not ripe for a return to the commune, so they would stay in a boarding house. They would do a bit of touring around in the jeep even though he knew it would not be as meaningful as touring in Enlightenment. Then after a while they would return to Fat Les's arch. He and Davey would have been working day and night and have built a very special machine. Then Ishmael and Marilyn would drive off together into infinity, or at least, if she really insisted, as far as Fox's Farm.

They said their goodbyes. Ishmael and Marilyn checked into a boarding house. It was a warm, clear day. They decided to go to the nude beach and take some LSD.

'Take some paper with you,' Marilyn said. 'You might want to make a few notes.'

*

Renata returns home. Her home is what she supposes a career-woman's flat is supposed to look like. It is a studio apartment with modern furniture in primary colours, polished boards, a hand-coloured print of a '57 Chevy on the wall, a fair number of books, most of them read, a chrome drinks trolley, a discreet colour television, a hi-fi, a black venetian blind.

She has been sent a record by a group calling themselves the Glove Compartment. The picture on the sleeve shows a photograph of the Ford works at Dagenham, and an elegant female hand holding a cocktail glass. Renata pours herself a tumbler of apple juice and steels herself to play the record. The music is young, brash, and not particularly in tune. A reedy teenage voice sings:

> When I'm feeling troubled
> When I'm not feeling free
> There's a weight on my shoulders
> And it's bothering me,
> I go down to the garage
> And I turn the key
> Then I drive like a bastard
> In my Ford Capri.

Ah well, she can give it an honourable mention in the news column. It could easily fill two or three column inches. But there are more pressing matters. She needs to wash her hair, do her nails, phone her mother and come up with thirty more things that you always wanted to know about the Volkswagen Beetle.

Ishmael's notes.
1 p.m. Call me Ishmael.
   The beach.
   The sun.
   A few nude people – mostly men as a matter of fact.

1.30 p.m. The beach.

The sea.

The sun has gone in a bit.

Fewer nude people. One man has been staring a little unpleasantly at Marilyn but she doesn't seem to object.

2 p.m. I say to Marilyn, 'Have you taken LSD before?'

'A few times.'

'Will it be fun?'

'Not fun exactly.'

'Will it be a learning experience?'

'Everything is a learning experience.'

The sea.

The beach.

The sun's come out again. Not much seems to be happening to my consciousness. Maybe it wasn't really LSD.

2.30 p.m. The beach.

The horizon.

The shape of the world is changed by the movement of pebbles.

The sky.

The DISTANCE.

Space that is limitless. Infinity in all directions.

We are each at the centre of the universe.

Looks like it really was LSD after all.

3 p.m. The beach.

Pebbles. They seem to move. They *do* move, of course.

The planet moves through space. Our bodies move in time to cosmic rhythms.

Bodies on the beach. Pale hieroglyphs. Their arrangement spells out messages when seen from above. A code? Who does the decoding?

3.30 p.m. All this time Marilyn's been reading a book. It has an Impressionist painting on the front. The colours move and vibrate. There is writing on the cover, but I can't read what it says. A code? What I *can* make out is a line of the blurb which says 'this unique book'. I shall have to think about that.

3.45 p.m. The sea.

In what sense can a book be said to be unique?

Printed matter, mechanical reproduction, unlimited editions. Not much uniqueness there.

'What makes a copy unique,' says Marilyn, 'is its position in space.'

4.30 p.m. Waves crash on to the shore.

The sky. The tides.

Lunar music that changes our positions in space.

5.15 p.m. The beach.

The wind.

The sun has gone in.

The beach is emptying. Ugly people. Grey sacks of flesh, open pores, moles that sprout hair. They speak out of the corner of their mouths. They talk dirty. They know something I don't. About the code? They put their clothes on. They put their skins on. Their skins are suits made out of a kind of rubber, very life-like, a substance not found in nature. Inside the rubber skin there is a form of life – part insect, part vegetable, and too loathsome even to think about. They are changing the shapes of space. Of course – that explains Marilyn's father's strange behaviour.

6 p.m. I am sitting in the Neptune Burger bar.

I felt a bit bad for a moment back there at the beach. Better now, except I have trouble holding my cup of coffee. It keeps changing size.

On the way here I saw a lot of parked Volkswagens. I counted them and noted the pattern.

The streets.

The Volkswagen stands at the crossroads of history.

As do we all.

7 p.m. I am sitting in a pub called the Green Man – fertility.

The beer tastes like urine.

The carpet.

The seats.

The juke box.

I'd like to hear some music from the road, from the spheres. The juke box is playing 'On the Blanket on the Ground'.

Things are getting jagged again.

Lads at the bar. Low-lifes. Smart, casual clothes. Always a bad sign. They're beautiful in their own way, but it is not my way. It is not the WAY.

The juke box has started playing 'My Way'.

I try to read their minds, their faces. It isn't hard. Their minds are full of bad chemicals. One day they're going to die. Why not today?

8 p.m. Still in the Green Man.

The effects seem to be wearing off. The beer glasses above the bar reflect light – it's just FANTASTIC.

I felt like taking my clothes off and standing naked so that the drinkers in the pub could see me as I really AM. Marilyn talked me out of it.

9 p.m. The beach again.

I am naked but my clothes are not far away.

Marilyn and I have just made love on a blanket on the shingle. Pebbles. Waves. EVERYTHING MOVED. It would. It has to. Oneness. Making love to a Goddess.

10 p.m. Back at the boarding house.

More or less back to normal, except for being very sensitive to noise from outside.

Who's making the noise? The Crockenfield Blazers?

I wish I could sleep, but every time I close my eyes there's an abyss. ABYSS. The window rattles. There are dark shapes just outside my field of vision.

The vibrations.

The wallpaper.

The fucking insects.

And do I trust Marilyn? After all, she is her father's

daughter. She carries the genetic code. She is also, of course, a Goddess.

From the street the sound of a Volkswagen. You can hear the state of the engine, the condition of the valves, the exhaust, whether it's a man or woman driving, his or her age, the state of mind, the state of the driver's soul.

Don't get too near the soul. That's where the insects live.

Nobody move.

Nobody say anything.

Get those insects out of here.

Beetles. Yes. Significant. Yes. Get it?

11.30 p.m. Marilyn is trying to help me 'mellow out'. She's given me red wine, orange juice and vitamin C tablets.

Or so she says.

Somebody fill that abyss will you?

Blood oranges, a breeding ground for maggots, dead dogs, bad souls. Welcome back to 'Sorrento'.

Nobody touch that light switch.

My flesh itches. Hair growing where it didn't grow before. Not hairs but legs. Spiders inside the skin, their legs sticking out through the pores.

Who's got the ray gun?

Who's got the nuclear device?

Let's blast those suckers.

They're going to have to die. Every one of them. All of us in the end, but some of *them* first. It's only a gesture but it's a start.

It's obvious.

Marilyn's father knew what he was talking about. He would. He's got his contacts. The time for talk is past. There are to be no prisoners. No surrender.

The slugs in the library. The velour tracksuit.

Kill the fuckers. Starting now.

Don't think I can write any more just at the moment . . .

*

121

The record continues,

> I wanna be free
> Don't need no more deception
> I wanna clean-living girl
> With no social infection
> I wanna Ford Capri
> That's got fuel injection.

Renata takes the record off before the fuzzed guitar solo cuts in. If they have ever written 'em like that before she suspects they won't be writing 'em like that very much longer. She turns the television on. There is a young black reporter standing in front of a wrecked car in a rural setting. The car could be a Range Rover. The reporter looks ill at ease, like someone only acting the part of a reporter, someone who has been hopelessly miscast.

He says, 'The sleepy village of Crockenfield was literally rocked last night. This house' (there is a shot of a large detached house with grounds) 'called "Sorrento" and owned by Mr Andrew Lederer was fire-bombed, cars such as the one behind me were set alight, there was a chase, shots were fired. Why?

'The attack was apparently motiveless, nothing was stolen and in the end nobody was hurt, although that in itself seems miraculous. And the only clue is that the attackers left the village in a supercharged Volkswagen Beetle.

'More curious still, I've spent most of the day here in Crockenfield and haven't been able to find anyone prepared to talk about the episode.

'Mr Lederer says he is too busy to speak to the media and claims it was merely youthful high spirits on the part of some of his daughter's friends.

'Where *is* his daughter by the way? And how is it that his attractive blonde wife managed to sleep through the entire episode?

'Here is Constable William Peterson . . .'

A tense young Constable speaks direct to camera.

'We heard shots, an explosion or two, and then we saw this Volkswagen leaving the scene at a hundred and twenty miles per hour. Basically we're baffled.'

Renata feels it would not take very much to basically baffle Constable Peterson. The reporter appears on screen again.

He says, 'Who fired those shots? Is there some strange vendetta that stalks the village of Crockenfield? Is there a political motive? And just who is hiding what from whom?

'This is Dudley Johnson, Kent at Six, Crockenfield.'

'Jesus Christ,' says Renata.

Later, Ishmael would be told that it can sometimes take years to recover from a particularly bad trip. In his own case he was unable to leave the boarding house for a few days. Marilyn was a tower of strength. She sat with him a lot, stroked his head, brought him food, and tried to talk him back to normality.

Renata tries to remember more about her hitch-hiker. She recalls the leather jacket, the ghetto-blaster, and some talk of a friend who was mad on Beetles, then a lot of nonsense about a damsel in distress. If she were a real newshound, a real pro, she would be on the phone, in her car, solving the mystery, getting the story, getting a scoop, getting on in her career. If she were even a decent, concerned citizen she would phone the police and give a description of her hitch-hiker.

What she actually does is take a piece of paper from her bureau and scrawl on it:

FACT: The sleepy village of Crockenfield was rocked earlier this month when the home of Mr Andrew

Lederer was mysteriously fire-bombed. Police were baffled. The only clue was that the attackers were driving a hot Volkswagen Beetle.

What the hell? She was never claiming to be Norman Mailer. She goes into her bathroom, turns on the immersion heater and decides to leave the phone call to her mother until another day. She decides she needs something stronger to drink than apple juice. She looks at what she has just written.

'Only another twenty-nine facts to go,' she says contentedly.

Marilyn had done a marvellous job of reasoning with the landlady of the boarding house. She explained Ishmael's loud behaviour, his screams, his breaking of the bathroom mirror, and his loudly proclaimed threats to blow up Brighton with his psychic powers, by saying that he had been in the Falklands and had a close friend blown up by an Argentinian mine. She knew the Falklands didn't have the same cachet as Vietnam but nobody could have mistaken Ishmael for an American vet.

The landlady was pacified at least for a few days. Then Ishmael developed the habit of waking at three in the morning and screaming 'Kill the parasites'. The landlady put up with it for three nights, and the intensity of his screams was considerably lower by the third night, but then she threw them, very politely, out.

Many girls would feel they had made a mistake if they were taken from home in a petrol-bombing raid and finished up in a Brighton boarding house looking after an acid casualty. Not Marilyn. She took it all in her stride. She took a lot of notes. Ishmael would lie on the bed, listening to the traffic noise, while Marilyn filled reporters' notebooks with very small handwriting. She had a feeling it might be useful later.

*

The putty features of Marty Feldman stare out from a newspaper ad for Volkswagen. The skin is grainy, the mouth soft, the eyes pointing to different corners of the page. The ad asserts that since Marty Feldman is extremely ugly his success must be based on talent alone – just like the Volkswagen. Not just a pretty face.

But it's worth remembering that Feldman's is a comedian's face and that a certain ugliness is something that many comedians trade on. Marty Feldman would not have become a successful romantic star, however talented.

Then again, another Volkswagen ad is headlined, 'After a few years, it starts to look beautiful.'

Bill Bernbach has other things on his mind. He is working on a campaign for the second most successful car-hire company in America. Second most, second best, are hard concepts to sell in America, but he manages – 'We try harder.'

Ishmael and Marilyn were sitting in the cab of the jeep.

'What do you want to do? Try another boarding house?'

'OK,' Ishmael replied.

'Would you like to go to Hastings? Lewes? Day trip to France?'

Ishmael shrugged.

'Anything you like,' he said.

'I know,' said Marilyn. 'Let's go to Fat Les's garage. You could see how they are getting on with rebuilding Enlightenment.'

Ishmael smiled.

'Yes,' he said. 'I'd like that.'

'It'll do you the world of good,' said Marilyn.

They were both wrong.

Eight

Steve is working at the White Oaks Petrol Station off the A30 in Dorset. It's rural. There's a big sign up that says 'We Serve You'. That's how rural it is.

In America, he thinks, it would all have been different. In America the job would have had some dignity. 'Pumping gas' sounds like a decent job. It even sounds romantic. The American words seem so much better, they sound so much more exciting. Trunks, hoods and fenders don't sound nearly so trivial as boots, bonnets and bumpers.

Steve has never worked in a petrol station before. He finds it all right. It's dull but it's easy. There isn't much to remember. If anybody tries robbing the till you let them have the money. You mustn't take a lump out of anybody's paintwork with the petrol nozzle. And you have to make absolutely sure than nobody uses the toilet who hasn't bought petrol.

People either treat him like dirt or as if he is a mechancial genius. Either way he has a lot of very dull conversations with customers. He tries hard but it all comes down to the same old things, 'Fill her up?', 'Nice car', 'What kind of mileage do you get?' It's very dull.

Marilyn drove the jeep. She had to take a very indirect route to avoid going anywhere near Crockenfield. They drove via Dartford, through the tunnel. They went round the M25 and up the M11 into Cambridgeshire. They drove past the motel where Marilyn had shown Ishmael her tattoo. They went to a family restaurant just off the motorway and had a bread roll with honey while the musak played 'Somewhere Over the Rainbow' and 'The Best Things in Life are Free'.

They went within a few miles of Fox's Farm and considered visiting the commune but they were too eager to get to Fat Les's Vee-Dub kingdom.

In his mind's eye Ishmael could see the railway arch, a collection of Beetles and Beetle parts, and in his mind's ear he could hear Wagnerian opera.

The reality, however, was somewhat different.

They drove along the mud track beside the railway arches, past a mass of weeds and a few derelict bits of motorcar. And there should have been a few parked Beetles and a big cheery hand-painted sign saying 'Fat Les – the Vee-Dub King'. But there wasn't.

Ishmael wondered for a moment if he had given Marilyn wrong directions and they had come to the wrong place, some other railway arch. Where the kingdom should have been there was only a mass of smoking wood and charred metal. Everything was burned black. Ishmael looked into the arch and could see the wrecks of two Beetles – one Enlightenment, the other belonging to Fat Les. Everything was destroyed.

Steve has a regular customer called Mr Kyle. He knows his name from his credit card. He is smooth, over-weight, with permed hair. He drives a Lotus.

'Shall I fill her up?' Steve asks.

Kyle grunts.

'Four star?'

'Well of course four star.'

'Nice car.'

'Just put the petrol in, son.'

Son? Steve is twenty-eight. He has a beard and the makings of a beer-gut. He knows twenty-eight is no age to be wasting his life serving petrol but when there's a recession on and you can't think of anything you'd rather be doing for a living, well, people think you ought to be grateful. Steve isn't grateful exactly, but a job's a job.

He dreams of meeting women in sports cars. He dreams they will be young, rich and delinquent.

He has hopes of one girl who buys petrol from him. She is short, wears a few articles of tight clothing and drives a Volkswagen Beetle cabriolet, the roof always down.

'Nice car,' he says.

'Yeah, isn't it?'

'I've always fancied a car with a soft top.'

'Soft top? Oh, we call them rag-tops or drop-heads.'

'You're American?'

'Afraid so.'

'That's fantastic.'

'What's so fantastic?'

'You know, American cars, freeways, Route 66. Fantastic.'

She smiles at him. He isn't sure if it's a real smile or just condescension. He convinces himself that it is real.

'Say, do you know anything about cars?'

'Yes,' he lies.

'Well when I brake, the car has a definite pull to the right. You know anything about that?'

'I think you'd better go to a Volkswagen specialist. Beetles can be tricky.'

'I guess.'

Steve spends the rest of the shift kicking himself. All right, so he didn't know anything about the brakes on a Volkswagen, but he could have bluffed. He could have offered to give the car a test drive and see exactly how bad the problem was, then after driving around with her for half an hour he could have asked for her phone number, *then* he could have told her to go to a Volkswagen specialist.

*

'Is this really where you've brought me?' Marilyn asked.

There was no sign of Fat Les or Davey. Ishmael and Marilyn went inside the arch, picking their way through the wreckage. There were charred girlie calendars, a smouldering tartan sleeping-bag. They held hands as they stood together in the ruins.

'Who could have done this?' Marilyn asked.

Then a voice behind them said, 'I've got one or two very shrewd ideas.'

It was Fat Les. He and Davey were standing outside the arch, wearing overalls, their faces and hair black with soot.

'It happened the night before last,' Fat Les said. 'I was asleep. I heard someone breaking in. I went to have a look. I got coshed. When I came round the place was on fire. They'd poured petrol everywhere and set fire to it. I could have been killed. I managed to drag Davey out. Just.'

Davey said, 'Everything's gone, everything. Someone's going to have to pay for this. Someone's going to have to be punished. Someone may even have to die.'

'You said it,' said Ishmael.

Steve finds the business with the toilet a large and complex joke. Jerry, the garage owner, is obsessed by it. He has had a vast lock fitted to the toilet door and the keys are kept behind the till in the office. Sooner or later the keys are bound to get lost or somebody will use the toilet and then accidentally drive away without giving the keys back. But Jerry is adamant – nobody gets to use the toilet unless they've bought petrol, not even if their bladders are rupturing and they've offered to write you into their will.

Steve finds it a little small-minded, but he doesn't need an argument with Jerry and, after all, there is an occasional grim satisfaction to be had from denying people.

Most of Steve's job satisfaction is at this kind of level. For instance, he becomes wonderfully satisfied after being obnoxious to Kyle. Kyle always uses his credit card. Steve writes out the chit as slowly as humanly possible, looks very closely at the signature, and often phones the credit card company for authorization.

It drives Kyle insane.

One day Steve tells him his Lotus needs new tyres.

'You're an expert on tyres as well as everything else, are you?' Kyle says.

'I don't need to be an expert to know that.'

'Look, your job is to serve the petrol . . .'

That does it. That always does it. Steve turns white with barely controlled anger.

'Don't tell me what my fucking job is,' he shouts. 'Don't ever fucking do that.'

Kyle realizes he has hit a vital spot. He shrugs his shoulders and stops telling Steve what his job is.

Steve almost begins to look forward to Kyle's arrival, to see if he can invent some new way of being difficult. He doesn't understand why Kyle keeps coming back, unless of course Kyle has started to enjoy the game as well.

'Do you think your father did this?' Ishmael asked Marilyn.

'He's capable of anything,' she said.

'Seems a bit extreme . . .'

'These are extreme times,' Marilyn replied. 'The world is an ugly and savage place. The rules have changed, perhaps there aren't any rules any longer. Husbands war with wives, parents are set against children. Politicians are set against all of us.'

'You said it,' said Ishmael. 'I'm sorry about your father but he's going to have to pay, he's going to have to be punished. He may even have to die.'

'It's the times we live in,' said Marilyn.

They stood in the smouldering ruins. Fat Les looked sadly at his burned possessions, but his eyes were bright with rage. He looked like a fallen hero. Davey fondled a tyre iron. He looked like a young warrior. Marilyn, at least to Ishmael, looked as much like a goddess as ever. They all looked at Ishmael.

'Follow me,' he said.

At least the American girl keeps coming back. One day after Steve has put in the petrol and she has started the engine again, Steve says, 'That engine's running much too fast.'

He's been rehearsing this.

'How's that?'

'The idle's too fast. You're wasting petrol, not doing your engine much good.'

'If you say so.'

'I can fix it.'

This is true. Adjusting the idle on a Volkswagen is one of the few mechanical jobs Steve can tackle with confidence.

'Is it a big job?' she asks.

'Ten-second job.'

'In that case . . .'

He fiddles with the idle adjustment and the engine settles down.

'Do I owe you anything?'

'Don't be silly.'

'Well that's kind of you.'

'What's your name?'

'Cindy.'

'Amazing. Really all-American. What do you do?'

She gives him a look as though he has asked her to explain relativity.

'I mean, what does anybody do?' she says. 'I run around in circles mostly, don't get anywhere, try to make

131

sense of it all, try not to get too burned out. I drink too much, do too many drugs. You know – the usual.'

'Sure. The usual,' Steve says.

She drives off.

Ishmael never had many friends when he was at school. He never made friends at work. But it never seemed to matter all that much. He was comfortable. He lived at home. He read books and watched television. He went out with Debby. Friends never seemed important.

Now life was uncomfortable. He didn't have his parents to hand, didn't have a job, didn't have books or television or Debby. Yet here, when he might have been at his lowest ebb, when he was most lost and alone, he had found himself among friends.

A lesson there, he thought.

Steve, what does *he* do? He works. He watches television, plays his records, drinks and generally wastes his life. It seems the obvious thing to do.

They know him in the local pubs, that is they know him as the one who arrives early, drinks too much and leaves late. One lunchtime he arrives at the pub and sees a Lotus parked outside. It belongs to Kyle. It is unlocked, the windows are wound down and the key is in the ignition. Steve reaches into the car, removes the key, puts it in his pocket and goes into the pub. Kyle is drinking gin and tonic at the bar. They ignore each other. Steve has a few drinks down his end of the bar. Kyle has a few down his. Kyle says goodbye to Tom the landlord and goes out to his car. Then he comes back.

'Tom, give me that phone. Get me the police. Some bastard's made off with my key.'

Steve looks up and makes a sympathetic face. While Kyle is phoning Steve leaves the pub, puts the key back in the car's ignition and goes home. It might have been interesting to see what happened if and when the police arrived but it is safer to leave.

Another time he sees Cindy's Beetle in the car-park of a steak restaurant. It is late. He has, naturally, been drinking. He is feeling quite self-confident. He finds a piece of paper in his jacket and writes on it, 'I AM ONLY A POOR PETROL-PUMP ATTENDANT BUT I LOVE YOU' and sticks it under her windscreen wiper.

Another day Jerry wants to see him. Steve is not hard to see.

Jerry says, 'I've been hearing that you were a bit out of order with Tim.'

'Who's bloody Tim?'

'Tim Kyle – he owns the video shop.'

'Does he? I always wondered what he did besides giving me a pain in the arse.'

'He tells me he had a bit of bother with his car keys. I think you know what I'm talking about.'

'I might know what you're talking about, but I don't know *why*. If Kyle's got something to say to me, he doesn't need you as a messenger boy, does he?'

'Don't push your luck, sunshine.'

'Tell Kyle not to push his.'

Male aggression – what a joke, thinks Steve.

'I thought we might be able to avoid any unpleasantness,' Jerry says.

'You thought wrong.'

Somebody needs serving. Steve goes and serves them. That's his job.

They walked the few miles to Fox's Farm. The ironies of this weren't lost on anyone. It just seemed appropriate.

'When you ain't got nothing, you've got nothing to lose,' Ishmael said as they walked.

'Sometimes I feel as though I'm living through a modern-day myth,' said Marilyn.

133

And all the time they walked Ishmael was thinking. All the time he was working out a plan – The Plan. He would need to be very persuasive, but he knew he had it in him.

The first member of the commune who saw him arrive was a tiny blonde woman whom he had hardly spoken to on his previous visit. She was thrilled to see him. She kissed him. She bounced up and down. He seemed to have made her day.

'You came back,' she shouted excitedly. 'We hoped you would. In a way we *knew* you would. This is where you belong. We need you. You are the sunshine of our lives. Wait till I tell the others.'

The evening meal at Fox's Farm was a great occasion. The other members of the commune were every bit as delighted to see Ishmael as the tiny blonde woman was. John the Hippy made a speech of welcome. Everyone else was still pretty sullen but they were obviously making an effort, and by their own standards they were embarrassingly warm. They were friendly, admiring. They were downright worshipful.

Sausage and beans and mashed potato were served for dinner. The communards constantly asked Ishmael if things were good enough for him. He said it was all fine. They were very concerned. He could have anything he wanted – more beans, brown sauce, anything. At first he found all the attention overwhelming, but it didn't take long for him to get used to it.

He made a short speech. He knew it wasn't great. It was a bit too general. He talked about the problems of the world today, the need to stamp out evil and capitalism, about the lack of spiritual insight, the misguidedness of middle class values, the lack of communication between people, and the fact that the devil incarnate was alive and well and living in a house called 'Sorrento' in Crocken-field.

He didn't feel that he was at his dynamic best, but it all

seemed to go down very well. Later he would tell them The Plan. For the time being they knelt at his feet and he placed his hands on each of the members of the commune in turn.

A few weeks pass. Steve has had enough. It is September. It is getting cold. He doesn't want to be standing on the forecourt all winter.

Then one day Kyle comes back. It is seven in the morning. The place is quiet. Steve is running the station on his own and has nearly finished his shift. Kyle pulls up at the pumps.

'I suppose you want petrol,' Steve says, doing his best to sound insolent.

'It's full of petrol,' Kyle says. 'I just want to use your toilet.'

'Jerry wouldn't like that,' Steve says.

'I've already had to speak to Jerry about you once.'

'*Had* to?'

'Just do your bloody job and give me the key to the crapper.'

Steve can see Cindy's Volkswagen about to pull into the petrol station. He has to think quickly. He enters the office, gets the toilet key and gives it to Kyle. Kyle goes into the toilet and the door closes itself behind him. Steve gets a tyre lever and jams it in the door so it won't open. He gets a container of brake fluid and empties the contents over the bonnet, wings and doors of the Lotus.

Cindy has pulled in and is waiting for petrol. She looks like she's been up half the night crying. Steve starts pumping petrol into her car. He can hear Kyle struggling with the toilet door, trying to get out. The tyre lever won't hold him long. Steve puts the nozzle back in the pump and screws the petrol cap back on Cindy's Beetle.

'You've hardly put any in,' she says.

Steve opens the passenger door and slides in beside her.

He can see the paint on the Lotus already starting to curdle. He can see the toilet door about to burst open.

'I think we'd really better get going,' he says to Cindy.

'Am I supposed to know what's going on here?'

'Better if you don't.'

Cindy smiles thinly, turns her eyes to the sky and she drives off.

'Am I supposed to know where we're going?'

'Better if neither of us do.'

They both laugh. They drive in silence for a long time, then Steve says, 'This is a really nice car. What kind of mileage do you get?'

Here, in a nutshell, as described by Ishmael to the members of Fox's Farm commune, is The Plan.

He said, 'There are times when it is necessary to make a gesture. There are times when it is necessary to perform a symbolic act.

'What do I want my gesture to symbolize?

'What act do I want to perform?

'I want to symbolize truth, beauty, goodness, love, light – the usual. I want it to symbolize a triumph over evil, complacency and middle class values.

'Are you with me so far?

'The problem – how to find a gesture and an act so powerful, so resonant, so rich in implication, that it can carry and communicate this weight of meaning.

'Can we blow up the Houses of Parliament? No.

'Can we cause civil disturbance? No.

'Can we surround an American Air Force base? No.

'Why not? Because what is needed is something more aesthetic, more creative, more domestic. More me.

'I have looked into myself, I have become my own myth. I have plunged down into my own self and I have dredged up from these lower depths the raw material I need for this heroic deed.

136

'I think naturally of Enlightenment – a charred hulk, consumed by the fires of evil.

'I think of Marilyn's father – a dark one if ever I've met one.

'I think of the Crockenfield Blazers – the serried forces of darkness unless I'm very much mistaken.

'It all seems very clear to me now. Marilyn's father and his cronies represent everything that is wrong in this vale of tears, everything that is evil and corrupt and middle class. They dwell in darkness.

'I know that we must confront that darkness. Let us throw down a challenge. Let us unite ourselves.

'We will meet them and fight them. Good and evil. Day and night. Heaven and Hell. God and the devil. Me and Marilyn's father.

'And if we are beaten? And if we are destroyed? So be it. But at least we'll have made our point.

'Symbolic acts are like that.

'It may not be the final solution, but it'll do for now.'

Nine

Ishmael and Marilyn and Fat Les and Davey stayed at the commune. Ishmael did his best to contribute to commune life but it's hard to fit in when people insist on treating you like a messiah.

It didn't worry him, though, since he was heavily concerned with the fine detail of The Plan, as, at one time or another, were most of the other members of the commune. Otherwise they ate, sulked, took drugs and went to work just like ordinary people.

John the Hippy was much as he had been when Ishmael had met him before except he had been using Marilyn's father's American Express card to modest but good effect. He now wore a pair of hand-tooled cowboy boots, a quartz wrist watch, a silk shirt in flame red, and he carried a top of the range Sony Walkman.

Eric was the name of the tie-wearer who had eventually told Ishmael how to get to Fat Les's. Eric didn't get spectacularly less sullen in the time it took to put The Plan into effect and Ishmael learned that he had a career in computers, all of which confirmed his opinion that Eric might not be the man for the big occasion.

The Norton twins, by contrast, looked very handy lads to have on your side. They were probably two very different and very individual boys, but they didn't seem to be. In fact, Ishmael could never tell one from the other. You might have called them Hell's Angels, certainly they were bikers. They rode big British motorcycles – Nortons, although Ishmael never discovered whether they were actually called Norton or whether that was just a nickname because of the bikes they rode.

They had pot-bellies, beards and long hair and were not the most approachable of people. They didn't seem to do much except ride their bikes, drink beer, and show their contempt for a pleasingly catholic variety of things – the police, 'straight' society, personal cleanliness, the family, drivers of MGs, newspapers and television.

Ishmael sort of liked them.

Tina was the tiny blonde woman who had been so glad to see Ishmael return. She looked about thirteen but could have been forty. Whatever her actual age, she had the distinct air of a runaway. She was very worshipful to Ishmael and he couldn't help wondering if she liked oral sex.

Caroline was the woman with the nose stud who had talked of being lost. She was very lean, usually carrying some kind of vegetable. Ishmael might once have thought that she had grown it herself organically, but now he assumed it must have been bought at the nearest hypermarket.

'Are you still lost?' he asked her.

'I don't know,' she said. 'I don't know if I know anything anymore.'

Mary was the artist. Every commune has to have at least one. She was interested in what you might call natural imagery. Her paintings usually featured the sea and the moon, mountains and suns and deserts, not that they looked like any deserts or mountains or seas that you'd ever actually come across, so Ishmael assumed they had to be symbolic.

He could see there would be a role for her in The Plan.

Harold was sixty. He looked like a derelict bank manager who had dropped out, and that was exactly what he was. He'd taken early retirement and decided to become a hippy. He wasn't all that much of a hippy. In fact he was another tie-wearer. Sometimes he even wore a suit, but if he did he was sure to subvert the effect by also wearing sandals or hiking boots.

Despite or because of his banking background Harold thought The Plan was a real winner.

There were others who came and went – a white-haired woman who cut everybody's hair, a pair of teenage punkettes, a Rastafarian in jogging gear who played the harmonica, a couple of used-car salesmen, a female plumber with hair to her waist. They were a chequered crew, but they all saw the good sense of The Plan, and they all loved Ishmael and would follow him anywhere.

Dawn breaks on the morning of 12 September 1974. It is New Year's Day according to the Ethiopian calendar and in the abandoned Imperial Palace Haile Selassie I listens to the throb of truck engines and the rumble of tank tracks as these vehicles pull into the palace grounds.

It has been a long time coming, this revolution, this deposal by the Provisional Government.

The Emperor receives three battle-dressed soldiers in one of the palace's less opulent chambers. One of the soldiers reads the act of dethronement, citing despotism, corruption and old age. The soldiers are calm. Their charges are restrained. The ceremony is bloodless.

Haile Selassie is led from the palace and assured that he will be conveyed to a safe place. He is accustomed to being driven in limousines, at the sight of which loyal subjects throw themselves to the ground, but today there is to be no such pomp.

In the driveway is a green Volkswagen Beetle, its engine running, an officer at the wheel. The officer leans over, shoves open the passenger door and tilts the front passenger seat forward so that the Emperor can get in the back.

Until now Haile Selassie has behaved with quiet resignation but this is too much.

'So it has come to this,' he protests. 'Is this really how I am to make my exit? Can you be serious?'

The final indignity.

Money is the problem. Haile Selassie died leaving perhaps a hundred million dollars locked in Swiss bank accounts. It is there still. Sometimes money can be come by very easily, all you need do is find a wallet or shit on a glass table. There is money for nothing. There is money for which you work your balls off. Ishmael worked hard at the library. Of course he knew it wasn't hard work like mining, or labouring on a building site, but to get up every morning and go to a job he hated – that was hard. And the money was nothing.

The Plan required money. It had to be stolen.

When the war ends Nina still considers herself a young woman, and a few years' deprivation has whipped her body to an erotic leanness it never had in the thirties. She even has high cheekbones these days; and dark eyes, and lips and nails the colour of blood. Dressed in tight black lace she sits at a scratched Steinway and sings 'These Foolish Things'.

A lonely, one-man-operated, twenty-four-hour self-service petrol station. A Volkswagen camper pulled into the forecourt and Ishmael got out. He filled the petrol tank. The camper was from the commune and full of people. They looked as though they were on their way back from a party. There was a festive atmosphere and fancy dress and party hats were in evidence. Ishmael went into the office to pay and to engage the cashier in friendly conversation.

Ishmael knew that the people who work as petrol station cashiers these days are either teenage boys or ageing men who have seen better days. In another economic climate they would have respected, steady jobs. They would have futures. But now there's a recession and they settle for what they can get. Sometimes they even have to pretend to like it.

This time there was a solid family man behind the counter. In another life he might have been a cheery milkman, but tonight he wasn't cheery and it probably wasn't just tonight.

'How are you?' Ishmael asked.

'So-so.'

'Nice night, eh?'

'Depends what you're doing.'

'What would you rather be doing?'

'Sleeping. At home. With the wife.'

'Night shifts must be hard.'

'You should try it.'

Ishmael looked around the office as if he were about to compliment the man on what a nice place he had here, but he didn't. He said, 'Do you know what the French word for petrol is?'

'Is this a quiz?'

'*Essence*. Pretty essential if you see what I mean.'

He didn't see what Ishmael meant. Ishmael laughed. The cashier didn't.

Ishmael said, 'Do you ever look into your heart and ask what's most essential to you?'

'No.'

'You should. Try to work out what things are worth living for, and what things are worth dying for.'

This produced a smile on the face of the cashier. People do sometimes smile when they start to get frightened.

'I'll bet you get some crazy people in here,' Ishmael said.

'Not until tonight.'

'Not until tonight,' Ishmael smiled. 'So how much do I owe you?'

The cashier smiled, this time with relief, thinking that Ishmael was getting down to paying, getting down to business, and in a sense he was right. Ishmael *was* getting down to business.

'Eighteen pounds,' he said.

'Did you say *eighteen*?'

He repeated, 'Eighteen.'

'Anyone would think I'd got money to burn.'

Ishmael laughed again.

He said, 'How long would a man like yourself have to work before he earned eighteen pounds?'

'About six hours, on a night shift.'

'That's a long time.'

'You're making it seem longer all the time.'

Fat Les and Davey and Marilyn and Eric and Tina then entered the office. Davey had shaved his head and was bare-chested except for some chains and a few streaks of oil. He looked dangerous. They all started examining the motor accessories, the key rings, the tins of oil and de-icer. Eric helped himself to a Mars Bar and handed out packets of cashew nuts and chewing gum.

'Have you ever been robbed?' Tina asked.

'Not until tonight,' the cashier replied.

'I could see you were an intelligent man,' said Ishmael.

Davey stood over the cashier, Fat Les emptied the till and Ishmael made a short speech.

'I'm sorry,' he said, and he did sound genuinely sorry. 'We're only stealing this money because we need it and because it's in a good cause. We mean no harm, but we'll smash your brains out if you get in the way of The Plan. I'm sorry you've got such a rotten job and I'm sure you've got enough problems without my adding to them, but these are hard times for all of us. Personally, I don't see any political solution to human misery, all that seems a bit simplistic – I mean when you didn't have a job you probably thought a job would solve all your problems,

143

but now you've got a job and you know it hasn't. Still, that's just a personal view. However, I do know that there are ways out. There are some roads that give smoother rides than others, and take you nearer to where you want to go. I found *my* road and I believe that it's within all of us to find it. And remember that a pocketful of truth is worth all the bulging cash registers on earth.'

Fat Les shut him up. Tina planted a kiss on the cashier's cheek, and the robbers piled into the camper and returned to Fox's Farm.

The Plan continued in this way. Two or three petrol stations a night, picked at random and all distant from each other, was enough to finance The Plan, though there was little left over for frills. Sometimes the cashiers were less philosophical than others but they were fortunate in not meeting any heroes. Ishmael supposed that heroes were reluctant to accept jobs in petrol stations.

What foolish things is Nina reminded of? Prostitution that became increasingly heavyweight as the war went on. When you will sell your soul for a pair of nylons, what price the body? And then the Yanks arrived – revaluation.

She supposes she's a survivor, perhaps even a winner. In England Richard Huntingdon has had a second highly-praised book of poems published. They speak of love in sufficiently ambiguous terms to be acceptable to most sexual preferences. Nina's so-so English will not enable her to determine whether there is some trace of herself somewhere in the poems, but she feels that surely there must be.

In Buchenwald Peter Baldung has shot himself in the head, but inexpertly, the bullet has done some damage but not enough and he is now in hospital with only enough brain left to allow feelings of intense well-being. Another winner.

Most foolish thing of all, Nina still has her Volkswagen

savers' card. She even managed to fill it. With the revalued Deutsch Mark her savings would be paltry enough, but imagine her anger and frustration when she learns that the 280 million Marks belonging to the savers were lodged in the German Labour Front's Bank in Berlin, and that the bank has suddenly found itself in 'East' Berlin and that the Russians have taken the money as reparations. Now would that have happened with the British?

Nina has difficulty knowing on whom to vent her anger. On Hitler? On the Nazi Party? On Russia? She feels her anger will not make much of an impression there.

But how about the newly constituted Volkswagen company? How about Herr Nordhoff?

Sunday lunchtime at the Castle Hotel, Crockenfield. Huddled in a corner, in a cloud of pipe and cigar smoke, talking urgently in hushed voices, are Marilyn's father and half a dozen of the Crockenfield Blazers. Normally they position themselves expansively at the bar, order doubles and exchange anecdotes that confirm their rugged, mannish, world view. But today some shared hurt has made them introverted and hushed. A plaque on the pub wall above their heads reads 'You are a stranger here but once'.

Money, freedom, power, the old trinity – the power and freedom to buy friendship, status, sex, to jump queues, to buy the 'better' things in life. If you've got it . . .

What did Ishmael spend his stolen money on? The basics. He bought Volkswagen performance parts, modified engines, paint, old wrecks of Beetles that needed complete restoration, welding equipment, bullet-proof glass.

Fat Les set up a kingdom in exile in the outbuildings of Fox's Farm. He could be found there most hours of the day or night, welding and tuning, stripping down and rebuilding, modifying and reconditioning.

Rupert says, 'It's not just the money, though God knows Range Rovers don't come cheap, it's the thought of being beaten by a rabble, a few oiks, yahoos. That's what really hurts.'

'There were more than a *few*. There were twenty or thirty at least.'

'And we weren't beaten exactly. We gave as good as we got. We ran them out of the valley after all.'

'Don't talk rot, Colin. They left when they heard the police sirens. We were thrashed. We were trounced and piddled on.'

'So they must have had military training – probably a bunch of renegade ex-marines.'

In October 1948 K-d-f savers formed an association to battle with the reconstituted Volkswagen company over the reclamation of their lost contributions. It would be thirteen years and a few days before the legalities were settled by the German Supreme Court. Savers who still held their completed cards could receive six hundred Deutsch Marks off the price of a new Volkswagen saloon (about £50), or they could take a hundred Deutsch Marks in cash.

Nina takes the money and buys a few bottles of wine. Tonight she is seeing her new boyfriend who works in the construction business. They will drink a bottle or two and go driving in his Opel Kadett.

Every day Davey would go out shopping and return with heavy-duty shock absorbers, fan shrouds, oil coolers, forged crankshafts, state of the art performance heads, ductile iron rocker arms, titanium racing valves, sidewinder exhausts, unswept extractors, manifolds, sway bars, roll bars, and chain-link steering wheels.

It was money well spent.

'If nothing else, I hope it teaches that wife of yours to keep the back door locked in future.'

Marilyn's father has been staring into his malt whisky. He has been silent till now, though not subdued, more possessed of an unearthly calm. He has been savouring the memory of his one-man attack on Fat Les's kingdom.

Now he says, 'I don't know whether she'll learn or not. For some people it may already be too late. But for those of us with eyes to see, it all gives a pretty clear picture of the state of things.'

'Sorry, not sure I'm quite with you.'

'Those who aren't with me are against me. It's a beginning, only a beginning. There are forces abroad in this great country of ours, they go by many names – the working class, the unions, the media, blacks, feminists, anarchists, militants, Jews . . .'

'Oh come off it, some of my best friends . . .'

'Well perhaps not Jews then, but certainly the rest; they're on the move, they're at battle stations and we're their target – the solid middle class, the decent folk, the entrepreneurs, the backbone of England.'

'Thank God we've at least got the students under control these days.'

Marilyn's father continues, 'They want us. They want to spit on us, to crap on everything we stand for. It's time to get fit, to arm ourselves morally and physically. There'll be fighting in the street, rivers of blood I shouldn't wonder. There'll be winners and losers. I know which side I intend to be on.'

'Well, I suppose you ought to know.'

'Yes I did. I do. So, are you with me or are you against me?'

They all agree that they are provisionally with him.

'All I can say,' says Robin, 'is that I'd like another crack at them, whoever they are.'

'I'll say.'

'Hear, hear.'

'I'll drink to that.'

They all agree that they'll drink to that.

'I think there'd be a very different outcome if it ever came to a rematch.'

'There will be a rematch,' says Marilyn's father. 'There will come a time. I feel it. I know it. And I'll be ready.'

'Rather.'

'I'll say.'

They agree that they'll be ready. Shooting practice and keep-fit sessions are arranged, along with cross-country running, weight training, and research into survival techniques. Pipes are filled and relit. Another round of drinks is ordered. They decide they need something a bit stronger this time.

And then, one day, The Plan was ready to sweep into its final phase. That was when Ishmael made his fateful phone call to Marilyn's father.

'Be gentle with him,' Marilyn said. 'But not too gentle.'

Ishmael made the call.

In August 1955 Heinz Nordhoff holds a jamboree to celebrate the production of the one millionth Beetle. Journalists arriving at the Wolfsburg factory receive a dupliacted copy of his speech. It runs to twenty sides and concludes: 'Hard work and determination has always been the strong point of the Germans, for we enjoy working if we know for what purpose, and I should think that everyone who has lived through the last fifteen catastrophic years really does know for what purpose.'

'Oh really?' thinks Ivan Hirst.

*

The last time Ishmael had seen Marilyn's father he had been standing in the drive of 'Sorrento', wearing a dressing-gown and wellingtons, carrying a shotgun and surrounded by walls of flaming petrol. How strange to think that Ishmael had once hoped to 'communicate' with him, and how much stranger to think he was now about to do it by telephone.

The phone rang for a long time before Marilyn's father answered.

'Yes?' he said at last, his voice sounding distant and high-pitched.

'Hello,' Ishmael said.

'Who is that?'

'I think you know who this is.'

'No I don't. Stop playing silly buggers.'

'Call me Ishmael,' said Ishmael deliberately.

There was a chilled silence at the other end of the line. Marilyn's father said, 'I knew you'd be in touch eventually. I've been preparing myself.'

Ishmael said, 'I don't think you'll be prepared enough.'

Marilyn's father said, 'How prepared do I have to be to deal with vermin?'

Ishmael said, 'If you think you're dealing with vermin then you've already lost.'

'I don't lose.'

'This time you do.'

They went on like this for a while longer, talking like villains in a comic strip, both believing themselves to be the good guy, occasionally laughing harshly, or bitterly as the situation demanded. It was a bit stilted.

'And what of Marilyn?' her father asked at last. 'Is she with you?'

'Yes she's here,' Ishmael said. 'She's fine.'

'Wasn't that all you wanted? Didn't you ought to be satisfied?'

'No,' Ishmael snapped. 'The game has changed. It's no

longer a game. The stakes are higher, and they're no longer material. Now they're spiritual.'

'I know that,' Marilyn's father said.

Ishmael said, 'We want to meet you, all of you, all the Crockenfield Blazers. We want to be at the centre of the cyclone. We want to be at the heart of the cancer, to be face to face with the heart of darkness. We are many and our hearts are clean. We are coming to pluck out the disease. We will arrive soon. We come with the best possible intentions – to destroy you.'

'We are ready,' said Marilyn's father. 'Now and for ever.'

The phone went dead.

'He got the message,' Ishmael said.

Saturday 16 June 1973, Malcolm Buchanan 'drives' his Beetle from the Isle of Man to England. He knows that the Beetle is famous for being waterproof and airtight, that it pays to open the window before trying to close the door, but this is a special sea-going version. Malcolm manages to travel thirty-two miles in just over seven hours, though he runs out of fuel just four hundred yards from the Cumberland coast. Now there's an existential image for you – a man alone, drifting across the sea, powerless to control his fate, in a floating Volkswagen Beetle. The car at last drifts ashore at St Bees Head. Malcolm tells the press he did it all for charity.

The Plan swept into its final mobile phase. Four Beetles stood outside Fox's Farm, but these were not ordinary Beetles. Fat Les and Davey had performed a transformation or two.

The windscreens were bullet-proof, the cars had monstrous all-terrain tyres, bumpers made out of steel tubing, hub-caps featuring Boadicea-style spikes, engines so big they burst from their compartments. Sheets of ugly, tattered metal had been welded on here and there as protective shields. They were ugly, deformed and dangerous. Mary had painted them with symbols – mandalas, eyes in pyramids, crescents, pentacles, yin and yang signs, swastikas – holy symbols.

And there was a fifth Beetle. It was Enlightenment and it was changed. Every inch of it was now black. Every piece of chrome had been removed. Bumpers, door handles, wheel centres, exhaust pipes, were all matt black. The headlights had black covers. The windows were smoked glass. Enlightenment sat low and vicious on fat tyres.

Ishmael sat inside, Marilyn beside him. It felt like home.

Fat Les drove the first of the other Beetles, Davey another, the Norton twins another, and Harold the former bank manager the fourth. Other members of the commune were scattered among the passenger seats, front and rear. They wore scraps of leather and animal skins. Their bodies and faces were painted, some heads were shaved. They carried axes and picks, claw hammers, sling-shots and Bowie knives.

They looked quite decorative.

Five engines burst into violent life. Ishmael led the grim procession out from Fox's Farm, out on to the roads, God's own country.

At his home in Yorkshire, nearly forty years after his time at Wolfsburg, Ivan Hirst straightens his cravat, lights his pipe, buttons his cardigan, and dusts his collection of model Beetles. It is probably the world's best collection and contains just four items.

He had the idea of a promotional toy or paperweight in the shape of the car as early as 1946, thus he was surely the first to confirm the Volkswagen's status as *objet d'art*. The first attempt at casting in aluminium was very crude and Hirst found it unacceptable – today it looks like a bar of soap in the shape of a Beetle, a bar that has been used several times. The second attempt was far more successful – wheels, doors and windows are clearly described in the aluminium. He kept an example of each of these two states of model on his desk until he left Wolfsburg in 1949.

It was an easy journey. They drove in stately procession with Ishmael at the head. They drove with due care and attention. They obeyed speed limits. They signalled clearly and in good time. They had consideration for other road users. They did not want to draw attention to themselves.

Two hours later they approached Crockenfield. They were ready. They drove along Hawk's Lane. They looked for ambushes. They looked for Range Rovers. They saw nothing.

Then they saw 'Sorrento'. They sounded their horns – five notes that refused to harmonize. They saw the wagon wheel gates. The gates were open. Ishmael slowed Enlightenment down to a crawl and drove into the grounds. The four other Beetles followed. They were ready for traps. They were ready to fight. They were as ready as they ever would be, but they found nothing.

There were no cars parked in front of the house. There was nobody at any of the windows. There was no servant woman telling them they couldn't park there.

They parked. They sat. They waited. They kept their engines running and their horns blaring. It seemed silly after a while. Ishmael turned off his engine. He stopped sounding his horn. He wound down his smoked window.

'Supposing they held a war and nobody came,' said Marilyn.

Ishmael opened his door. He stepped out. His torn blue leather creaked in the warm, still afternoon. He felt scared, yet he felt ready. He had three days' growth of beard. He looked the part.

He walked to the front door and rang the bell. Nobody answered. He wasn't surprised. He turned the door handle. It wasn't locked.

He looked back at the other Beetles. Doors were now opening, people were getting out. Marilyn and John the Hippy and Fat Les walked towards the house.

'It's got to be a trap hasn't it?' said John the Hippy.

Ishmael still didn't know. They entered the house. It was still and silent and nicely furnished. In the sitting room Marilyn asked whether anyone would like a drink from her father's cocktail cabinet. They declined.

They searched the house. It was empty. It was ghostly, like a show house, inhuman and unlived-in. They sat in the kitchen. They felt uncomfortable. Other road warriors entered – Davey and Harold the former bank manager and Tina and Eric the tie-wearer and Caroline with the nose-stud and Mary the artist. They made cups of coffee. They tried to make themselves at home. They were not sure whether they were experiencing victory or defeat.

Should they loot and destroy the house? Should they just go home? Where was home for Ishmael now?

'We could set up a squat, I suppose,' said Eric the tie-wearer.

'It reminds me of one time I went to Margate,' said Fat Les. 'The fuzz had got the whole place carved up. We never even got a look at the rockers. I didn't have a decent bit of bother all weekend.'

Ivan Hirst also owns a unique model of a Beetle-based Reichspost truck, and a one-tenth scale saloon, just like one Adolf Hitler is photographed holding, but this one comes from Heinz Nordhoff. Nordhoff would gladly have given Hirst an actual Beetle cabriolet, but Hirst's military position prevented him from accepting.

So Hirst has his models to dust, his spoils of war. They are a better way of remembering than most. They speak of creation and of rebuilding. History resides in them as much as in scars, in tattooed skins, in ruined lives and cities, in documentary photographs that need constant reinterpretation.

Today Ivan Hirst drives a BMW.

The Norton twins were standing outside the back door, keeping the garden watched. Suddenly they moved very quickly and entered the house. Ishmael looked out of the kitchen window. There were ten or a dozen men in tweeds, advancing through the herbaceous borders with shotguns.

Suddenly there was a knock on the front door.

'Do we answer it?' Tina asked.

'Of course we do,' Ishmael said. 'It's quite usual for opposing war lords to hurl a few insults at each other prior to the fray.'

He went to the front door. Harold the former bank manager opened the door for him. He was ready for a confrontation with Marilyn's father, with the devil himself if it came to that. But even so he was surprised to find a uniformed police constable on the doorstep.

'Hello sir,' the policeman said. 'My name's Constable Peterson and I just happened to be passing when I couldn't help noticing those rather unusual motors parked outside. We're having a little bit of a campaign in Crockenfield right now and unless I'm very much mistaken each of those cars is failing to display a valid tax disc. I trust you do have tax, sir, and I'd also be very much obliged to see your driver's licence and a current MOT certificate, sir.'

Ishmael was unsure whether this was a real police constable or whether this was some elaborate ruse by Marilyn's father. Either way Ishmael wanted to be rid of the pest.

'Go away,' Ishmael said gently.

'I beg your pardon, sir?'

'Go away please or you may get hurt.'

'I'll pretend I didn't hear that.'

'Then hear this. We are on a mission. Forces of good and evil are here in confrontation. Darkness and light will here collide. I don't think this is a police matter.'

'With respect, sir, I think you'd better let me be the judge of that. I suppose you have proof that you actually own those cars?'

'Listen, little man,' Ishmael said. 'You are out of your depth. Be warned.'

'I think I'd better step inside and ask you a few questions, sir.'

At that moment a volley of shots was fired from the rear of the house. The windows in the kitchen shattered with a good deal of sound and fury.

'Be gone,' Ishmael commanded the policeman.

Constable Peterson ran away at some speed. As he did so he almost bumped into two Crockenfield Blazers who were advancing on the house from the direction of the front gate. All three were mutually shocked. One of the Blazers dropped his shotgun and the constable accelerated his exit.

His parting remark was, 'I'll be back and I won't be on my own.'

Ishmael had to agree with Clausewitz about war being like a fog, certainly he remained vague about what happened in the next ten minutes. But he knew for certain at the end of that time that there was not a pane of glass left in any of the windows of 'Sorrento', all of them having been shot out by Marilyn's father and his chums, and the whole crew of them were occupying the grounds looking frantic and drunk on blood lust. In the same time the whole of Hawk's Lane that ran in front of 'Sorrento' became blocked by police cars, motorcycles, fire engines, ambulances and sightseers. Ishmael couldn't help thinking that things weren't quite going to plan – The Plan.

There is a photograph of Ferdinand Porsche taken by his nephew and secretary Ghislane Kaes some time after his release by the French. It shows Porsche leaning on the door of a Beetle parked at a gravel roadside in the Grossglockner, Karnten, in Porsche's native Austria.

There are mountains in the distance. There is a sharp drop from the edge of the road, down to what could be water, though in the photograph it appears jet black.

Porsche could be staring away to the distant mountains, he could be looking at something on the water beyond the edge of the photograph; but it appears to us now that his stare is unfocused, and that his posture shows weariness, not relaxation. Other eyes could interpret the photograph as that of a man on holiday standing beside a new car of which he is very proud, but our eyes interpret it as a defeated man staring at nothing.

This interpretation can, of course, also be interpreted.

And so it was that Ishmael and his followers found themselves besieged in Marilyn's father's house, surrounded by a large number of Crockenfield Blazers who were in their turn surrounded by ever increasing numbers of police.

Harold the former bank manager suggested that they make a foolhardy charge at the Blazers and go out in a blooming of fey glory, but he didn't get any support. Even Ishmael thought it was too symbolic by half.

A plain-clothes police officer stood at the gates to 'Sorrento' and made a more or less inaudible speech about this all being madness and they'd all regret it later, and everything could be smoothed out over beer and sandwiches with a little common sense.

The moment he finished there was a shot or two fired in his general direction and Fat Les lobbed an empty gin bottle at him through a smashed upper window.

Then Marilyn's father spoke. He was glassy-eyed and unsteady on his feet, and he spoke from behind a rhododendron bush, though with, Ishmael would have been the first to admit, an undeniable authority. He denounced the police, the state, youth, Ishmael, the two-party system, the courts, the internal combustion engine, and finally women. His final remark was that unless the police kept their distance there would be a terrible blood-bath and he'd slaughter everyone.

Obviously, Ishmael couldn't let such an opportunity slip by. He stood at an upstairs window and bawled out a few generalizations about natural law, life and death, the road, and transcendent love.

It was well received by his followers who naturally then turned to him for guidance in their hour of need.

'I'm all for a bit of a confrontation,' Fat Les said. 'But I can't see much percentage in slugging it out with these Blazers if we then have to take on the pigs.'

Ishmael looked deep into himself. He felt tired. He felt old. He felt a long way from home and as though he'd lost all his maps. It was not, to begin again, what he had expected. He remembered how much he abhorred violence, and suddenly, like the protagonist of a thriller who gets a second bump on the head and wakes saying, 'Who am I? Where am I? How did I get myself into this mess?', he had his best idea yet.

He said, 'I think I'll hold a press conference.'

'Why a press conference?' Marilyn answered.

'Because the tv camera is mightier than the sword, and we don't have any swords, and because I think I'll be rather good at it.'

'You think so?'

'Yes. I have an easy and winning manner. I say what I

mean, I don't get tongue-tied, and people listen. I mean I convinced all you lot.'

'Yeah,' said Eric the tie-wearer, sullenly. 'You know, rather than a confrontation with the devil himself I might be prepared to settle for getting out of this unscathed, unarrested, and sloping off down the pub.'

Typical.

'And will they want to interview you anyway?' asked Davey. 'I mean, we're not exactly national news, are we?'

'I think we are,' Marilyn said. 'You see, what I haven't told any of you is that my father, as well as being insensitive, brutal and slightly insane – he's also a Conservative MP.'

You could have heard a pin drop if it hadn't been for the police sirens and the occasional random shot. Les was the first to speak.

'You mean we kidnapped a politician's daughter, fire-bombed him, and then took over his house.'

'Yes,' said Marilyn.

'Why the fuck didn't you tell us?' Fat Les shrieked.

'If I'd told you you wouldn't have gone along with Ishmael's plan.'

'Too bloody right.'

'Then I wouldn't have any material for my novel.'

'We'll have the fucking army after us.'

'I should think so,' said Marilyn.

'I think we're more than a match for the army,' said Harold.

'Oh shut up, you old prat,' said Fat Les.

'Hey,' said John the Hippy. 'This is getting heavy.'

'Bollocks,' said the Norton twins as one man.

'How about that,' said Davey. 'Fancy me getting my leg over with an MP's wife.'

'WHAT?'

'When I got Marilyn out, well I couldn't find her room at first. I finished up in the missus's bedroom and she

158

wouldn't let me go till I'd given her one. She seemed well pleased.'

'Oh sweet Jesus Christ,' said Fat Les.

'Please don't worry,' said Ishmael. 'I can talk us out of this.'

Ten

Adolf Hitler says, 'Without motorcars, sound film and wireless [there is] no victory for National Socialism.'

There are only winners and losers, good guys and bad guys. Ishmael began as a convincing bad guy – the crazy in the customized Volkswagen, the raider, not appealing, not prime time. Marilyn's father made a very acceptable good guy – a property owner, a company director, a businessman, an MP defending his territory and principles. And that was how the events were reported at first. Then Marilyn's father tried to shoot an Independent Radio News sound crew who were recording an interview with Constable Peterson. Then he was the bad guy. Then they wanted a hero, so they wanted to talk to Ishmael. They wanted him to be lovably eccentric and an underdog with his back to the wall.

The Berlin Bunker. Jung called it 'a dark reflection of a universal symbol in the collective unconscious of our culture', but then, he would. It conjures up images of stained, bare concrete, a tiny enclosed cube, a pill-box in the ruins; and we see the Führer, lonely, mad, isolated, perhaps finally heroic, going down with his city, pacing like a menagerie animal, wielding a revolver, spouting his political testament; the last man in a ruined world, the last sleeper in a dream that has died.

Outside 'Sorrento' there was a group of photographers

and cameramen and reporters, all jockeying for position by the front gate. In full view of these people Ishmael and Marilyn opened the front door, stood on the step and shouted that they wanted to talk to them. Marilyn stood in front of Ishmael as a shield, banking on the fact that while her father might be happy to slaughter reporters, police and hippies, he would hold back from shooting his own daughter. Ishmael was not certain that this was anything to bank on, but he was eager to face the press.

The Bunker is the Berlin Chancellery air-raid shelter. It is a two storey construction, built fifty feet beneath the ground, the lower storey being Hitler's domain – eighteen rooms set along a central corridor, six of them a suite for Hitler and Eva Braun. Eva has her own bed-sitting room, bathroom and dressing room. Hitler sleeps in a separate room. And there is a map room, a study, a telephone exchange, guard rooms, and a space containing a generator. There are also two rooms for Goebbels, and a room for Stumpfegger – Hitler's latest surgeon.

On the upper floor Goebbels' wife and his six children occupy four rooms, there is a kitchen, the servants' quarters, and a dining room. There is also accommodation for Heinz Linge, Hitler's valet; his SS adjutant; Fraulein Manzialy, his vegetarian cook. And there are the dogs – Hitler's alsatian Blondi has given birth to a litter and Hitler has adopted one, giving it his own nickname of Wolf. There are also lots of visitors from the neighbouring shelters – Bormann, Krebs, Burgdorf, Axmann.

The questions came thick and fast, shouted over the twenty-yard gap between the house and the front gate. Ishmael answered calmy but loudly and clearly.

Q: Are you a terrorist? Are you part of a terrorist organization?

161

A: No sir, certainly not. Not a terrorist, not organized.

Q: But you do have followers?

A: I have a few friends with whom I travel the same road. But we're motorists, not terrorists.

Q: Why are they dressed in paramilitary uniform?

A: You call this paramilitary? I call it fancy dress.

Q: Then why fancy dress?

A: It's fun.

Q: Terrorists or not, is it true that you came here to attack the home of Mr Lederer?

A: Not true. We just stopped by for a bit of a chat. We came as pilgrims. He's our local MP, after all.

Q: You came to discuss politics?

A: I'm afraid politics is a bit low on the cosmic scale by our standards. I was after something higher. I wanted to discuss truth, beauty, love. You know, the real issues.

Q: How far did you get in your discussions?

A: Not very far I'm afraid. We came openly to his front door. We knocked, we entered, we thought perhaps Mr Lederer had slipped out for a moment and would be back soon. And in fact he was back soon but sadly he was in no mood for discussions.

Q: In fact he appears to have thought you were out to destroy his property and threaten his life.

A: I understand Mr Lederer has been working too hard.

The Bunker then, is a cramped crowded madhouse, but in Berlin in April 1945 it might not have seemed such a bad place to be. At street level the Russian air-raids continue daily, and soon the Bolshevik forces will be walking the streets of Berlin and perfunctorily sweeping aside what little resistance is still being offered by a few remaining German companies and some stragglers from the Hitler Youth.

Q: Let's get this straight, are you saying you came to

'Sorrento' to discuss spiritual matters and Mr Lederer and a group of his friends attacked you?

A: I couldn't have put it better.

Q: Unprovoked?

A: Well something must have provoked him, but it wasn't me.

Q: You seriously expect us to believe that a distinguished Member of Parliament would behave in this appalling way?

A: The road of expectations is a muddy track with potholes and black ice. I'd never met a politician until I met Mr Lederer but his mad behaviour seems fairly consistent with my impression of the average politician. (*General laughter issued from the members of the press.*)

Q: What do you know about the petrol bombing of Mr Lederer's house a few weeks ago?

A: Was it petrol bombed? I didn't know that. Perhaps that was part of the reason why he was so touchy. A thing like that's bound to be upsetting.

Q: So why do you think Mr Lederer attacked you?

A: That's easy. He's a maniac.

Q: What is the connection between yourself and Mr Lederer's daughter?

A: Our connection is spiritual, mental and physical. It's sublime. Love is the greatest thing. It's all you need. I'd like to tell all the viewers and listeners and readers that love is still alive in the world today. It may not be easy to stumble across but I've found it and so can they.

Q: Do you think Mr Lederer can find it?

A: What a very good question. Why shouldn't he? But it may take a lot of work.

Q: Would you still like to have a 'chat' with Mr Lederer?

A: Sure. If he'd listen.

Q: And if he listened, what would you say to him?

*

163

Eva Braun – we see a high contrast sepia photograph of a thick-waisted, naked woman caught in a dance pose, on a beach, under a streaked sky. She loves him. She has stood by her man. While Hitler was rising to power she was content not to be married. She didn't want to stand in the way of his career. Behind every successful dictator . . . In the Bunker that is no longer a problem. She arrived unexpectedly and announced her decision to stay with him to the end. Love and death thrive in the ruined city. It is pure opera.

A: I would say to him, 'Sir, politics is all very well in its place, but it's not the whole answer. We must go further, drive ourselves that bit harder. Let us be rally drivers of the human soul.'

Q: Is it true that you threw down some sort of 'challenge' to Mr Lederer and the Crockenfield Blazers?

A: There is one challenge I throw down and it is this: I challenge you to find the light. Look into God's fog lamps and try not to be dazzled. Pluck out the cat's eyes of darkness. Replace the flattened battery and the dulled parking lights of evil.

Hitler is fifty-six. He celebrates his birthday in the Bunker. It is a low-key affair. Karl-Otto Saul gives him a finely-detailed scale model of a 350mm mortar. Everyone admires the gesture. Hitler tells how the previous day he was having some blood drawn from his arm in the hope of relieving a venomous headache. The blood blocked the hypodermic needle, spurted, and had to be caught in a beaker. 'All we needed to do was add some fat and some seasoning and we could have sold it as Führer blood sausage.'

Q: Is it true you used to be a librarian?
A: Yes.

Q: Why did you give it up?

A: Because the repair manual of life is too large a volume to be contained in a single library.

Q: And tell us, what is the significance of the Volkswagen?

A: The Volkswagen is the Chariot of the New Gods.

And now Hitler and Eva Braun are to be married in the Bunker. Depending on your sources you may like to believe that Hitler is riddled with venereal disease, or that he is incapable of sexual intercourse, or, of course, both.

Not that it matters now to Eva, not that it matters much to anyone in Berlin any more. Walter Wagner, a municipal councillor wearing a party uniform and a Volkssturm armband, conducts the wedding ceremony. It takes place in the Bunker's map room. The couple pledge that they are of pure Aryan extraction, though Hitler of course is lying. Eva wears the black silk dress that is Hitler's favourite. Goebbels and Bormann are the witnesses. Afterwards they retire to drink champagne and talk about the past.

Ishmael was beginning to be the good guy. All right, so he'd lied through his teeth, but there is more than one way to defeat the forces of night, more than one symbolic act that can be performed. And he knew that he'd handled the press with considerable panache and charm, and as he stood there addressing his public, with reporters hanging on his words, recording them and writing them down, he felt very at home.

Night fell. The siege continued. The police trained lights on the house. Marilyn's father and the Crockenfield Blazers were quiet for most of the night, but they would let off occasional random shots to show they were still in business.

Inside 'Sorrento' the siege victims gathered round the television. Recordings of Ishmael's interview were on every bulletin. He watched himself with pleasure. He was somewhat masked by Marilyn and the sound was poor, but taking all the difficulties into consideration, he thought it was great television.

The media were now telling a simple and appealing story. Ishmael and his followers, whom the television news had dubbed the Children of Enlightenment, or even C of E, were harmless but eccentric zealots who had popped in on Andrew Lederer just at the very moment that he had gone completely off his head and started wanting to shoot everything in sight. If a passing policeman hadn't raised the alarm there might well have been an orgy of death.

Fat Les sat in a swivel chair, drinking neat gin, and reflected that the part about the orgy of death was all too true, and he knew whose death it was likely to have been.

After a clip of Ishmael speaking there was a studio discussion with a couple of MPs and a psychiatrist and they offered the opinion that with the pressure of modern politics being so extreme it was a wonder that some politician hadn't snapped before now.

Renata and Max, her current – for want of a better word – lover, sit on Max's tubular steel settee. They have drinks, joints, and a hand inside each other's clothing. It is late. The *Abbey Road* album is on the stereo and they are watching, as they often do, a sample from Max's extensive collection of blue videos.

Night passed slowly in 'Sorrento'. Ishmael talked with Fat Les.

'You know,' Fat Les said, 'I think we were all fucking insane to be conned by your glib tongue in the first place.'

'You weren't conned,' Ishmael replied calmly.

'What could we have hoped to achieve? How could we have hoped to take on this lot? They're armed for Christ's sake!'

166

'Winning and losing aren't the only issues. Win or lose it would still have been symbolic.'

'Symbolic, my arse.'

'You had your free will, Les. You didn't have to do what I asked.'

Max adjusts the contrast as the film, which has no titles, shudders into life. There is an external establishing shot of a supermarket. A young, wholesome-looking girl in a fur coat is seen to enter. We enter with her and see her wandering between the rows of merchandise, selecting items and slipping them under her coat. The camera lets us glimpse that she is naked beneath the coat – well, functionally naked, naked but for the high heels, suspender belt and stockings that this genre demands.

She selects items carefully for their phallic nature – a cucumber, bananas, a bottle of ketchup. This goes on for a while until a man (a customer? store detective? supermarket employee? – the film fails to make this clear) begins to follow her up and down the aisles.

The glimpses of nakedness which were previously just for the camera are now directed at the man, and the girl becomes increasingly teasing and explicit. She runs the cucumber up and down her thigh and pokes it around in her pubic region. The man takes the hint and before long he is penetrating her with a handily shaped bottle of olive oil.

The girl comes to a rapid, faked, orgasm.

Dawn arrived on punctured tyres. Ishmael stood in the library with Davey.

Davey said, 'There's something I've got to tell you.'

'Go on, my son.'

'I know fuck-all about martial arts. I enrolled for the course all right, but the teacher slung me out after two lessons. The wanker said I didn't have any aptitude for the spiritual dimension.'

'Oh Davey, Davey.'

On the landing Ishmael met John the Hippy. He looked downcast. Ishmael asked what was the matter.

'I wish we'd never given you that acid,' he said.

Harold the former bank manager walked by.

'I still say we can make a fight of it,' he said.

'Bollocks,' said the Norton twins.

As soon as it was light there was another meeting with the press. It was less dramatic than the previous one. Ishmael said he'd passed a peaceful night and had scrambled egg for breakfast. He was lying. The reporters at the gate held up the morning editions of their newspapers. Marilyn and Ishmael appeared on the front pages of most of them and one headline read 'HOSTAGES OF LOVE'.

This time the reporters wanted to talk to Marilyn. She had washed her hair and done her make-up for the occasion. She said she still loved her father, that she thought Ishmael was a very unusual and interesting man, and that her ambition in life was to be a writer.

They appeared on both morning television channels, and there was film of the Crockenfield Blazers holed-up in various locations around the grounds of 'Sorrento', though there were conspicuously fewer this morning than there had been the previous afternoon.

Hitler's nights have been pretty ragged lately, and his wedding night is no different. There are conferences to be held, attempts made at establishing radio contact, plans to be discussed, fires of hope to be stoked, traitors to be denounced. He therefore sleeps little, and when he does so it is not until late the next morning. He eventually falls asleep at seven or eight in the morning to be woken a few hours later by the sound of renewed shelling. He gets up, dresses with the utmost care and correctness, then takes breakfast – coffee and a selection of cakes, chocolate, sponge – party food.

The morning after his wedding he is seated in his study, under a picture of Frederick the Great, waiting for his breakfast to be delivered. Fraulein Manzialy arrives with a tray which is covered by a pink gingham cloth. She removes the cloth with a flourish and presents Adolf Hitler with an exquisite chocolate cake in the shape of a Volkswagen Beetle.

There is a jump in the film and we now see the man and the girl riding in an open car. (Renata cannot fail to notice that it is a rather special Beetle cabriolet, in red metalflake with some tasteful black pinstriping.) On the back seat there are two boxes of groceries, and in the front seats the girl drives with one hand while manipulating her passenger's cock with the other. There is some rapid editing which offends exact continuity and before long, before very long at all, the man is ejaculating furiously and copiously, and there is sperm dancing across the dashboard, on to the windscreen, on the gear lever, everywhere.

The SAS arrived at 'Sorrento' at about ten in the morning. There were helicopters and men hanging from rope ladders and leaping on to the roof. There were smoke bombs, stun grenades and a few rounds of automatic fire. It all took about forty-five seconds.

Very little of the action could be seen from inside the house, but when some of the smoke had cleared it was possible to see Marilyn's father and half a dozen Crockenfield Blazers being led away, their hands up, their eyes watering, and surrounded by armed SAS men in flak suits with black bags over their heads. Marilyn's father was put in an ambulance and the others were loaded into a black maria.

Another cut. The car draws to a halt on the edge of a desert. There is sand and scrub. The girl lies on the ground

169

beside the car. This time she is *actually* naked – shoes, stockings and suspenders are nowhere to be seen. The man seems, curiously, to be fiddling with the groceries, and his reason now becomes apparent. He stands over the girl with an egg in his hand. He breaks the egg so that the yolk falls through the air and lands very precisely on the girl's left breast – a direct hit. More eggs follow until there is a film of albumen and broken yolks over most of her torso.

Events now progress rapidly. Via a series of jump cuts we see ketchup splashed around her neck and shoulders, chicken livers splattered across her thighs, honey coating her chin and cheeks. Baked beans, instant coffee, cling peaches, vegetable oil all follow until she is all but entirely clothed in this (more or less) edible silt.

The front door of 'Sorrento' was thrown open and a sea of people flooded into the house. Photographers, cameramen and reporters were at the front of the mob, closely followed by police. Behind them were the ambulance men, the firemen and the sightseers from the village, and finally there was a number of men in very sharp suits with very sharp haircuts, and guns spoiling the neat lines of their jackets.

Everything got filmed and photographed – Marilyn and Ishmael, alone and together, with Fat Les and Davey, with other members of the commune. The house got photographed – every room, including Marilyn's mother's exotic bedroom – the garden, the drive, the wagon wheel gates and of course the five Beetles.

Ishmael and Marilyn posed in front of Enlightenment and answered a few last questions. Marilyn took care of the bright, breezy banter, Ishmael restricted himself to hammering home the spiritual message. They made a good team. The media lapped it up. So did the crowd of well-wishers who had gathered.

'Finally, Ishmael,' a reporter from ITN asked, 'after all

that you've been through, what are your feelings about Mr Lederer?'

Ishmael thought long and hard.

'I forgive him,' he said.

The well-wishers cheered and one or two plucked up enough courage to ask Ishmael for his autograph.

The man is now naked and one would assume that he is about to lower himself on to the swamp of food within which there is the naked body of a woman. But that would be a hasty assumption. The camera focuses on his penis which is only semi-erect and slowly a stream of urine emerges. The camera follows its descent and roams over the areas of the girl's body where urine mixes with food and where a nipple or navel occasionally shows through. The girl does a reasonable job of pretending to enjoy herself.

So far the film has been unusual yet plodding. It is different from the run of the mill blue movie but there has been nothing spectacularly inventive, and nothing, as Max and Renata have been all too aware, spectacularly erotic. Certainly there has been nothing to prepare them for the extraordinary filmic coup that the director pulls off in the dying minutes of the film, a coup which completely transforms the base materials with which he has been working.

The man and woman, she still on her back, he finishing his pee, become aware that someone is approaching. There is a long shot of a stranger walking towards them. The man and woman register mimed alarm.

And then comes the master stroke.

The film suddenly switches into fast motion reverse. Urine streams back into the man's penis, ketchup leaps back into its bottle, eggs reform themselves. In less than a minute the groceries are whole and returned to the car. The girl is still naked but her body is perfectly clean and

171

she now (in forward motion) slips her fur coat on just as the stranger passes by. There is a final shot of the Beetle driving away along a desert road before the film ends.

The police wanted Ishmael and Marilyn to help them with their inquiries. Ishmael and Marilyn wanted to sleep.

'We were the victims of this siege you know,' Marilyn said. 'You're treating us like criminals.'

A man with a sharp suit and haircut said, 'No we aren't, madam. We just hope you'll be able to clear up one or two matters for us.'

'Any objections if we go to a motel?'

'None at all, madam, so long as we know which one.'

Ishmael said, 'I've had it with motels, this time I'm going first class.'

'Really, sir?'

'Really. If anybody wants us we'll be at the Kensington Astoria.'

He'd heard the name on a radio programme. They took Davey as their chauffeur. At first Ishmael felt uneasy about letting anyone but himself drive Enlightenment, but now that he was going first class it seemed appropriate.

'What are you going to do when you get to the hotel?' Davey asked.

'I'm going to wait for offers,' Ishmael said.

'Pornography is like pastoral poetry,' says Max. 'It must fulfil certain inviolable conditions. The rules are set. The requirements are rigid. To be inventive within that strait-jacket of form is the mark of the true genius.'

Renata sips her drink and doesn't say anything. She has heard Max's opinions on other occasions, knows them well, and feels that they result from too many years spent in the seminar room.

*

172

They arrived at the Kensington Astoria. Ishmael asked for a suite of rooms for himself and Marilyn, and a single room for Davey. The hotel was happy to oblige. They knew who their guests were. They were celebrities. They'd been on television. Nobody asked whether they had money. Nobody told them how much anything cost. The hotel staff just said what an honour it was to meet Ishmael.

The suite of rooms was a bit ostentatious for Ishmael's tastes. Everything was cream coloured and had mouldings. Ishmael headed for the bedroom.

'No, Marilyn,' he said, 'you can't be with me now. I need to be alone. You stay out of the bedroom and answer the phone. Tell them all I'm in conference but I'm prepared to consider all offers.'

He closed the bedroom door behind him, stretched out on the king-size bed and fell deep asleep.

When he awoke it was dark. From the sitting room of the suite he could hear a television, and Marilyn talking on the phone. He entered the room. There was mess everywhere. Marilyn was sitting on the floor amid an undergrowth of newspapers, letters, flowers, telexes, wine bottles, two video recorders and a number of telephones, two of which were ringing.

'The phones have been jammed all day,' Marilyn said. 'They all want you, Ishmael. It looks like you're a star.'

'Who wants me? And what for?'

'So far you've been offered radio spots on "Start the Week" and "Any Questions". They want you to read your favourite Bible passage on some Sunday religious tv programme. Radio One wants you to play your ten favourite singles of all time. You can be a guest on "Breakfast Time", "Celebrity Squares", "Call My Bluff" and "Blankety Blank".

'The *Observer* wants to discuss your being guest motoring editor. You've been invited to address the

Volkswagen Owners' Club of Great Britain – small time, perhaps, but probably worthwhile. The *Sunday Times* wants to do a Life in the Day and the *Sunday Express* wants you for their Things I Wish I'd Known at Eighteen. Oh and the *TV Times* would like you to take over their problem page.

'Then there are the people who are prepared to pay just for the pleasure of interviewing you. In the last half hour alone I've spoken to *Woman's Own*, *Penthouse*, *Fast Lane*, the *Church Times* and the *New Musical Express*.

'You can open supermarkets, endorse products, test-drive any car in the world, meet anyone you want to meet, have free tickets to anything, and you can have all the sponsorship anyone could possibly hope for.

'The tabloids all want to do your story, although they all want it to be exclusive; and David Frost and Terry Wogan have both said they'll be in touch first thing tomorrow.

'So what shall I do? Shall I start accepting for you?'

'No,' said Ishmael. 'I'm waiting for the big one.'

'Big one?'

'Yes, Marilyn. You and I deserve our own chat show.'

'Did you enjoy the film?' Max asks. 'Want to see any of it again in slow motion or freeze frame or whatever?'

'Very weird,' says Renata. 'What is it about Volkswagens?'

'Volkswagens?'

'The car in the film was a Volkswagen.'

'Was it?'

'You didn't notice?'

'Of course I didn't notice. I don't watch porn films just to look at the cars.'

'No, I suppose most people wouldn't,' she says sadly.

But she would. She does. She is no longer able to walk past Beetles without noting their year and model, the variations in headlight shapes, the flat and round windscreens, the presence or absence and distribution of engine air intake slots, the design and position of rear light clusters. And these are of course only the factory variations. There is also the whole world of modification, of personalizing and customizing. Anything that can possibly be done to a car has been done to a Volkswagen – endless variety, endless transformation – somewhat like pornography and pastoral poetry.

'Want to see another film?' Max asks.

'Later,' says Renata. 'Much later.'

From being besieged in 'Sorrento', Ishmael and Marilyn were now besieged in the Kensington Astoria. Two days passed. Reporters camped in the lobby. There were armies of fans waiting in the street. They were still hot news.

Men belonging to arcane departments of the police force came to interview them. It was clear they didn't for a moment believe the version of events that Ishmael had given to the media, but since Marilyn's father was still gently raving in some private clinic, and since Ishmael was now a public figure, they seemed reluctant to bring any charges. They hadn't worked out who had done what to whom, and they liked Ishmael's version of events more than any other they could think up.

Marilyn had a phone call from her mother. She had been staying with 'a friend' when all the trouble started. She had returned to 'Sorrento' to find every window smashed, police still in occupation, her husband locked up and her daughter on every front page in the land. She managed to take it very well.

In the next few days Ishmael and Marilyn met producers from all the significant television companies. They arrived in a posse and lounged around the hotel suite, all brief-cases and smart but casual clothes. Ishmael had trouble telling one from another.

'What kind of chat show are we discussing here?' asked one of them.

'Simple,' said Ishmael. 'Marilyn is in the studio with one or two newsworthy guests . . .'

'But Ishmael, old mate,' said a man with a cockney accent and a very expensive leather blouson, 'Marilyn is very young, totally untried.'

'That's the deal,' said Ishmael.

There was a grumbling acceptance of this, accompanied by the premonition that worse was to come.

'And I am "our man in a Volkswagen", "the man with Enlightenment". I roam the country in a Beetle meeting eccentrics, sages, idiot savants; having insights, and sharing my inner visions with the viewers.'

'Would you be on film?'

'No. I'd be absolutely live. There'll be a crew with me, hand-picked for their spiritual awareness, and they'd have to travel in Volkswagens.'

Brief-cases were snapped open, papers rattled, French cigarettes were lit.

'And how many nights a week are we talking about?'

'Five,' said Ishmael.

'And I suppose you're talking main evening slot.'

'Don't be silly,' said Ishmael. 'Do you think I want to be over-exposed? No, I think late night.'

'And how much money is this going to cost us?'

'Ah money,' said Ishmael. 'It's the root of all evil, you know. But if there are any of you who aren't offering half a million up front then I'll ask you kindly to leave my hotel suite.'

Nobody left.

'Right, gentlemen. Talk to me.'

And talk they did. In the end Ishmael accepted an offer from the BBC, not because it was the highest (it wasn't), but because he thought his mum would like that. He had been in touch with his parents, or rather they had been in touch with him, only briefly and only by phone. He had promised to buy them a detached bungalow. They said Debby was heart-broken. They said he was a heartless bastard and a bad son, and that he looked a daft sod in his leather suit. They hadn't changed. A prophet is always without honour in the Osgathorpe family.

Renata has long since completed her Volkswagen article, but the legacy is a pile of magazines containing articles on Volkswagens that Terry has given her. Some of it is dull stuff – 'D-I-Y servicing made simple', 'How to Cure That Flat-Four Flatspot'; but there are some issues of a magazine called *Cal Vee-Dub*. The title is newspeak, or she supposes illiterate-speak for 'California Volkswagen'. They do things differently there. *Cal Vee-Dub* is like a girlie magazine but with salacious pictures of over-polished Beetles and over-endowed engines instead of girls. And just as girlie magazines address their readers in a heated private language, so the descriptions of California-style Beetles are written in some coded style, curiously dislocated from any world 'out there'.

Ronnie DeVoto's '64 Vee-Dub is a real attention-grabber, super sano and clean to the max.

It took three years and four thousand dollars to convert a 1200cc clunker into the Looker you see today.

Brother Carl gets the credit for the trick paint-job – check out that sparkling Clementine orange and the wrap-around graphics.

The interior is decked out with buttoned naugahyde and brushed aluminum dash, while the sounds pound through a Uher 4-speaker system.

But this baby is for Go as well as Show. A Type 1 universal case is fitted with an 86mm Berg crank, Carillo 5.500 rods, 94mm Cima pistons and barrels, and Super Flo II heads.

We like it. How about you?

Renata supposes she does. Very much. Is she obsessed? she asks herself. Is it healthy? She has even started work on a new article called 'Fifty More Facts You Always Wanted to Know About the Volkswagen Beetle'. Her latest facts run like this:

TWENTY ITEMS THAT HAVE BEEN MADE IN THE SHAPE OF A VOLKSWAGEN BEETLE

Rings, key-rings, earrings, cakes, dice shakers, clocks, pens, ashtrays, soap dishes, belt buckles, radios, lamps, whisky bottles, pen-holders, staplers, telephones, bath mats, money boxes, paperweights, loo-roll holders.

FIFTEEN ITEMS THAT ALTHOUGH NOT SHAPED LIKE A BEETLE HAVE HAD PICTURES OF BEETLES ON THEM

Tee-shirts, sweat shirts, sweaters, underpants, blankets, lunch boxes, rulers, cushions, scarves, lamp shades, adhesive tape, tubes of glue, umbrellas, biscuit tins, postage stamps.

NINE ITEMS THAT SO FAR AS WE KNOW HAVE NEVER BEEN MADE IN THE SHAPE OF A BEETLE, THOUGH WE SEE NO REASON WHY NOT

Beds, wigs, electric guitars, fly papers, cameras, vacuum cleaners, umbrella stands, massage gloves, frisbees (although we admit that the Beetle shape might impair the frisbee's aerodynamic properties).

Perhaps this new article is getting a little baroque. And it's not as if she didn't have other things on her mind – lots of things. She still hasn't phoned her mother, she still needs a manicure, and she really does need to ditch Max. However, the main thing that's on her mind, and she doesn't know if this is the symptom or the disease, is this guy Ishmael. It all seems to tie in – the fact that she has written about Volkswagens, the fact that she gave a lift to one of Ishmael's 'followers', and more especially the fact that she expected them to get locked up when they are not only at liberty, but that Ishmael has become some sort of quasi-mystical folk hero, some symbol of something or other. He has captured, or at least hijacked, the public imagination.

Every time she's picked up a newspaper this last week or so he's been there, with his Beetle and his leathers and his MP's daughter girlfriend who wants to be a writer. It makes her angry. Yes, it all seems to tie in and in some way it involves her. It doesn't seem to mean anything but it all ties in.

Terry, of course, has told her to go along to the Kensington Astoria and get an interview, but Renata has told Terry that getting Ishmael to give an interview these days is about as easy as getting the Pope to model swim-wear.

And all this time she has the feeling that she has seen him (Ishmael, not the Pope) before somewhere, and she becomes increasingly convinced of this, though she gets no nearer to recalling where or when. She recalls visits to parties, press launches, motor shows, even to car-parks and libraries, it would have to be at that sort of place that she saw him, wouldn't it? She doesn't know. She still doesn't know as she phones her mother, and she still doesn't know as she paints her nails. And as she picks up the phone again, gingerly because the varnish is still wet, to phone Max, she still doesn't know.

But as Max speaks, as it flits through her mind that what she really wants to say to Max is, sorry this whole thing has just been a bad idea from beginning to end, all we have in common is drink, drugs and sex, at that moment she very suddenly and absolutely certainly *knows*.

'Max,' she says, 'I have to come over and see you right now.'

It was early evening. Marilyn and Ishmael sat together in their suite, taking a final look at the BBC contract before signing.

'It's going to be an awesome responsibility,' Ishmael said. 'I'm going to be very powerful, very well-loved, comparatively rich. I'm going to be able to change the world. I only hope I can keep my humility and the common touch.'

Marilyn poured him another glass of champagne. Late sun spilled into the room. All seemed well with the world. They were thinking that dinner wouldn't be long away, when there was a knock on the door. Naturally Ishmael was furious. He had instructed the management time and time again to make sure they had no visitors.

'Who's there?' Ishmael shouted angrily.

'It's me. Davey.'

Ishmael grudgingly opened the door.

'You might have telephoned first,' he said.

'Then you might not have seen us.'

Ishmael saw that Davey was not alone. There was a woman with him. She carried a notebook and a video cassette.

'All right then,' Ishmael said. 'Come in, but not for long.'

'This is Renata,' Davey said.

Ishmael said hello to Renata.

'Renata's a journalist,' Davey said.

'Oh for Christ's sake, Davey,' Ishmael yelled. 'I'm not seeing journalists at the moment. How many times do I have to tell people?'

'I think you'll see Renata,' Davey said, and there was a threat in his voice, a hint of 'or else'.

'Yes,' said Renata. 'You'll see me. And you'll see this videotape.'

The film, which begins without titles, is shot from one camera position. Occasionally the lens zooms in and out, although as filmic syntax the zooms fail to articulate anything. They're just done to relieve the boredom. The colour is bad, the lighting patchy, and the soundtrack non-existent.

The film shows a room which is elegant in a masculine sort of way – a few art deco objects, a lot of mirrors which manage to avoid showing the camera, a rattan three-piece suite and a nest of glass tables.

A bulky, middle-aged man is lying on the floor under one of the tables. He is wearing nothing but a leather dog-collar and a latex posing pouch. A second, younger, man is seen. He is removing a blue leather motorcycle suit. He walks awkwardly, reluctantly across the room to where the man and the table are. He squats above the glass top, his naked buttocks visibly straining to shit.

'Seen enough?' Renata asks.

'I've seen more than enough,' said Ishmael.

'Ishmael!' Marilyn shrieked. 'How could you do it?'

'It wasn't easy.'

'But how could you do this to me?'

'I didn't know you then.'

'Talk about feet of clay,' Davey sneered.

'I didn't know it was being filmed.'

'Is that supposed to make a difference?' Marilyn demanded.

'I never had you down for a shirt-lifter, I really didn't,' Davey continued.

'I never lifted my shirt,' Ishmael protested. 'I just took off my leathers. My heart wasn't in it. You could see that from the film. I was only in it for the money.'

'Some spiritual guide you turned out to be,' said Davey. 'Not just an ordinary shirt-lifter, but one who does it with shit for money.'

Marilyn said, 'Ishmael, I hope you realize it's all over between us, instantly and for ever.'

'Hey, don't go all middle class on me.'

'And what's wrong with being middle class?'

'Oh no,' Ishmael moaned. Had all his words been in vain?

Renata had been watching all this with barely restrained fury. 'Look,' she said, 'I know there are going to be a few broken hearts over this, but really I'm more concerned with the hordes of press and the "fans" who are out there dying for a chance to see you.'

'Is this blackmail?' Ishmael asked. 'How much money do you want for the tape?'

'I don't want money, and besides this obviously isn't the only copy of the tape.'

'And I'd make damn sure I found one,' said Davey. 'And I'd make damn sure everybody saw it and knew that their new chat-show host was a filthy pervert.'

'I'm at your mercy,' Ishmael said. 'Go on then, crucify me.'

'That won't be necessary,' said Renata. 'But I do have one or two ideas.'

It was just as well that Ishmael and Marilyn hadn't got round to signing the BBC contract. The BBC were understandably furious when Ishmael informed them that he wouldn't now be signing, and suspected some dirty trickery was taking place. But an anonymous note containing a still from the incriminating video arrived on the Director-General's desk one morning. The BBC were so relieved at their narrow escape that they promised Marilyn a job as a researcher after her graduation, and they assured Ishmael that there were no hard feelings.

Ishmael? He turned down every deal he'd been offered. He had to. That was one of Renata's conditions. He did no television, no radio, no interviews, endorsed no products, made no after dinner speeches. He did sell his story, however. He refused to deal with any writer except Renata Caswell of *Cult Car*. That surprised a lot of people.

A Sunday tabloid bought the story, paid well, and turned the story into a three-part serial. Ishmael didn't write it, of course. Renata wrote it and he put his name to it. He had to. The story must have sold quite a few newspapers since there was still lots of public interest in Ishmael, but the story was not quite the one that people wanted to hear. It contained the hot news that Ishmael was going to renounce the world. As follows:

> Today I don't wear leather. I shave every day. I eat healthfoods and I abhor violence. I suddenly found myself in a position of potentially awesome power. I could have become an idol, an international tv star, a leader of men. But I looked into my soul and something told me that this was not the way. I found I'd made a mistake. I realized that all this pop-religion I'd been spouting was so much drivel. I had been deceiving myself. I decided not to deceive anyone else.
>
> If I have any message left to give the world, it's this,
>
> > Don't follow leaders
> > Watch for parking meters.

Great advice even if it doesn't rhyme.

By 29 April 1945 Hitler has heard that Mussolini and Clara Petacci are dead and that their bodies are hanging in Milan's Piazzale Loreto. He will make sure that he does not end the same way. At the very end it is Erich Kempka, Hitler's chauffeur, who is ordered to send two hundred litres of petrol to the Chancellery garden to immolate the corpses of Hitler and Eva Braun.

Russian shells burst around the Chancellery, some unidentifiable figures stand in the garden, giving a Nazi salute. A sheet of flame leaps angrily, futilely at the sky, some failed emblem of escape.

At Fox's Farm a dozen or so sullen communards are eating

curried egg while watching television. Their eyes are intent but they see only patterns and shapes. They hear words but the words don't arrange themselves into comprehensible patterns. The curry tastes of everything and nothing. They are smashed out of their heads.

In one of the farm's outbuildings, behind locked doors, Fat Les has spent the evening lowering a tarted Cal-look Beetle. He starts the engine. The space begins to fill with carbon monoxide. It wouldn't be so hard after all. He turns on the car radio. There is a phone-in programme on Parkinson's disease. He changes station. No Wagner, instead there is The Who, 'Won't Get Fooled Again'. He turns off the engine. Not worth it for the sake of that little shit Ishmael.

An old man's hands on a steering wheel, the skin mottled with liver spots, the wheel bound in textured leather. Ivan Hirst parks his BMW in a lay-by on the A57. Cars go by. Pretty people. Tanks full of petrol, heads full of lager and materialism. In-car stereos pump out middle-of-the-road music. Ivan Hirst lights his pipe, unwraps a Yorkie bar. It's a full life.

Marilyn sits at her newly acquired word-processor. She is home from Oxford for the weekend. She is attempting to be a writer. Her fingers magic-up words on the screen.

To the Germans it is the Kafer, to the Dutch the Kever. Yugoslavians speak of the Buba, the French of the Coccinelle. But by any name be it Bug or Beetle, or Maggliolino, or Escarabajo, or Fusca, the Volkswagen sits at the crossroads of history, roads that lead to Auschwitz and Hiroshima, to the concentration camp and the atomic bomb site. And there at these crossroads stood I, hand in hand with Ishmael . . .

She hears her mother downstairs. A clink of glass, a

184

rattle of ice cubes. Mummy is making Martinis. Marilyn decides to join her.

Renata is the proud driver of a Porsche 911. She has handed in her notice at *Cult Car*. She doesn't know what career she will fail in next but she has enough money from the sale of Ishmael's story for this not to be a pressing concern.

Renata did slip Ishmael a few hundred pounds out of her fee. He used it to rent a caravan on a small site near Filey.

It was late in the year. The weather was cold and the rent was cheap. Enlightenment was parked beside the caravan. He didn't use it much any more. Sometimes he would sit in the driver's seat, the engine not running, his hands on the wheel, his mind full of old dreams. He was not 'home' but there was nowhere else he wanted to be.

He cooked simple meals on the Calor gas stove. Sometimes he walked by the sea. Sometimes he listened to the radio. Sometimes he read a motoring magazine. Time passed, but not quickly.

Then one day he was sitting on the step of his caravan when a red Ford Capri approached. It stopped at the entrance to the site and a woman got out. Ishmael knew her. He ought to have done. It was Debby. She had never looked better. She was fashionably dressed. She had had her hair done short and stylish. She had also evidently learned to drive.

'Debby,' he said, when she reached the caravan.

'Barry,' she said.

They touched hands and soon found themselves in a passionate embrace, holding each other desperately. They went into the caravan, took their clothes off and got into the narrow bunk.

And then Debby did a most uncharacteristic thing. Before Ishmael knew where he was there were torrents of

185

hot semen coursing like molten lava down Debby's moist, yielding, eager throat. She kissed him thickly on the mouth, leaving his lips streaked with his own sperm.

'Oh Debby,' Ishmael said. 'There was Mount Fujiyama in my own carport the whole time, but I had to travel very far before I knew where home was.'

'Barry,' Debby said after a moment's consideration, 'you do talk a lot of crap.'

That was the nicest thing anybody had said to him for a very long time.